1 MONTH OF
FREE
READING

at

www.ForgottenBooks.com

By purchasing this book you are eligible for one month membership to ForgottenBooks.com, giving you unlimited access to our entire collection of over 1,000,000 titles via our web site and mobile apps.

To claim your free month visit:

www.forgottenbooks.com/free589242

ISBN 978-0-267-37203-4
PIBN 10589242

THE BROWN STUDY

by

GRACE S. RICHMOND

The power of self-sacrifice is that it conquers the
heart, a citadel that is impregnable to weaker things
When you have tried all other weapons, try this
It is the sharpest sword in the arsenal of heaven.
—*From "The Fighting Saint"*
by James M. Stifler

Illustrated by Herman Pfeifer

GARDEN CITY   NEW YORK
DOUBLEDAY, PAGE & COMPANY
1917

... ... here? Did Sue leave it—or did you ... ...
the photograph, staring at it with ...

THE BROWN STUDY

by

GRACE S. RICHMOND

The power of self-sacrifice is that it conquers the
heart, a citadel that is impregnable to weaker things.
When you have tried all other weapons, try this
It is the sharpest sword in the arsenal of heaven.
—*From "The Fighting Saint"
by James M Stifler*

Illustrated by Herman Pfeifer

GARDEN CITY   NEW YORK
DOUBLEDAY, PAGE & COMPANY
1917

TO
THE LIVING MEMORY
OF
EDWARDS PARK CLEAVELAND

CONTENTS

LIST OF ILLUSTRATIONS

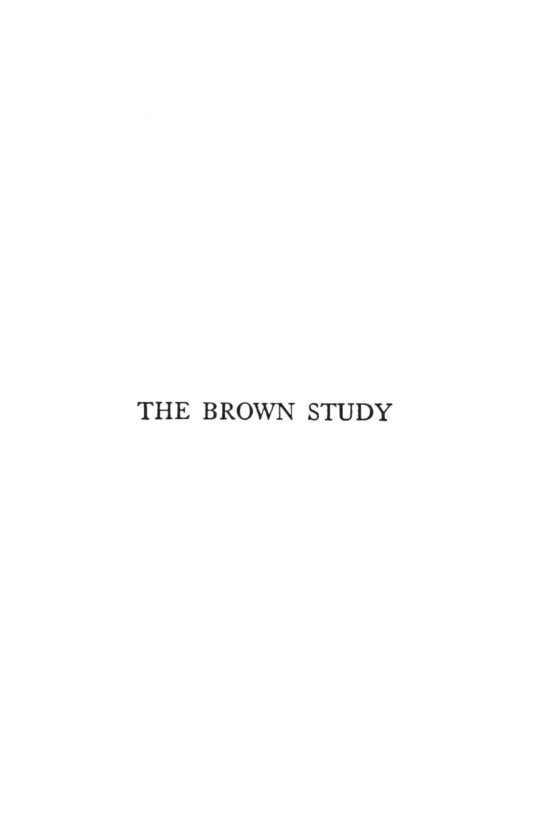

THE BROWN STUDY

I

BROWN HIMSELF

Brown was so tall and thin, and his study was so low and square, that the one in the other seemed a misfit.

There was not much in the study. A few shelves of books—not all learned books by any means—three chairs, one of them a rocker cushioned in a cheerful red; a battered old desk; a broad and rather comfortable looking couch: this was nearly all the study's furniture. There was a fireplace with a crumbling old hearth-stone, and usually a roaring fire within; and a chimney-piece above, where stood a few photographs and some odd-looking articles of apparently small value. On the walls were two small portraits—of an elderly man and woman.

This was absolutely all there was in the room worth mentioning—except when Brown was in it. Then, of course, there was Brown. This is not a truism, it is a large, significant fact. When you had once seen Brown in his study you knew that the room would be empty when he was out of it, no matter who remained. Not that Brown was such a big, broad-shouldered, dominating figure of a man. He was so tall and thin of figure that he looked almost gaunt, and so spare and dark of face that he appeared almost austere. Yet when you observed him closely he did not seem really austere, for out of his eyes, of a clear, deep gray, looked not only power but sympathy, and not only patience but humour. His mouth was clean-cut and strong, and it could smile in a rather wonderful way. As to the years he had spent—they might have been thirty, or forty, or twenty, according to the hour

in which one met him.   As a matter of fact he
was, at the beginning of this history, not very
far along in the thirties, though when that rather
wonderful smile of his was not in evidence one
might have taken him for somewhat older.

I had forgotten.   Besides Brown when he was
in the study there was usually, also, Bim.   Also
long and lean, also brown, with a rough, shaggy
coat and the suggestion of collie blood about him
—though he was plainly a mixture of several
breeds—Bim belonged to Brown, and to Brown's
immediate environment, whenever Bim himself
was able to accomplish it.   When he was not
able he was accustomed to wait patiently outside the door of Brown's small bachelor abode.
This door opened directly from the street into
the Brown Study.

The really curious thing about the study was
that nobody in that quarter of the big city knew
it was a study.   They called the place simply
"*Brown's.*"   Who Brown himself was they did

not know, either. He had come to live in the little old house about a year ago. He was dressed so plainly, and everything about him, including his manner, was of such an unobtrusive simplicity, that he attracted little attention—at first. Soon his immediate neighbours were on terms of interested acquaintanceship with him, though how they got there they could not themselves have told—it had never occurred to them to wonder. The thing had come about naturally, somehow. Presently others besides his immediate neighbours knew Brown, had become friends of Brown. They never wondered how it had happened.

The Brown Study had many callers. It was by now thoroughly used to them, for it had all sorts, every day of the month, at any hour of the day, at almost any hour of the night.

II

BROWN'S CALLER—ONE OF MANY

A caller had just come stumbling in out of the November murk, half blind with weariness and unhappiness and general discouragement. Brown had welcomed him heartily.

"It's nothing in particular," growled the other man, presently, "and it's everything. I'm down and out."

"Lost your job?"

"No, but I'm going to lose it."

"How do you know?"

"Everything points that way."

"What, for instance?"

"Oh—I can't tell you, so you'd understand."

"**Am** I so thick-headed?" Brown asked the

question seriously. His eyes, keen, yet full of sympathetic interest, rested inquiringly upon his caller's face.

"It's in the air, that's all I can say. I wouldn't be surprised to be fired any minute—after eight years' service. And—it's got on my nerves so I can't do decent work, even to keep up my own self-respect till I do go. And what I'm to do afterward——"

Brown was silent, looking into the fire. His caller shifted in his chair; he had shifted already a dozen times since he sat down. His nervous hands gripped the worn arms of the rocker restlessly, unclosing only to take fresh hold, until the knuckles shone white.

"There's the wife," said Brown presently.

The caller groaned aloud in his unhappiness.

"And the kiddies."

"God! Yes."

"I meant to mention Him," said Brown, in a

quietly matter-of-fact way. "I'm glad you thought of Him. He's in this situation, too."

The caller's brow grew black. "That's one thing I came to say to you: I'm through with all that. No use to give me any of it. I don't believe in it—that's all."

Brown considered him, apparently not in the least shocked. The caller's clothes were very nearly shabby, certainly ill-kept. His shoes had not been blackened that day. He needed a hair-cut. His sensitive, thin face was sallow, and there were dark circles under his moody eyes.

Brown got up and went out by a door which opened beside the chimney-piece into the room behind, which was his kitchen. He stirred about there for some time, then he invited Jennings out. There were crisply fried bacon and eggs, and toast and steaming coffee ready for the two men—Brown's cookery.

They sat down, and Brown bowed his head.

His companion did not bow his but he dropped his eyes, letting his glance rest upon the bacon.

"*Lord*," said Brown simply, "*we ask Thy blessing on this food. Give us food for our souls, as well. We need it. Amen.*"

Then he looked up at the caller. "Pitch in, Jennings," said he, and set the example.

For a man who professed to have had his supper Jennings did pretty well.

When the meal was over Brown sent Jennings back to the fireside while he himself washed the dishes. When he rejoined his visitor Jennings looked up with a sombre face.

"Life's just what that card a fellow tacked up in the office one day says it is: —'*one damned thing after another*,'" he asserted grimly. "There's no use trying to see any good in it all."

Brown looked up quickly. Into his eyes leaped a sudden look of understanding, and of more than understanding—anger with something, or some one. But his voice was quiet.

"So somebody's put that card up in your office, too. I wonder how many of them there are tacked up in offices all over the country."

"A good many, I guess."

"I suppose every time you look up at it, it convinces you all over again," remarked Brown. He picked up the poker, and leaning forward began to stir the fire.

"I don't need convincing. I know it—I've experienced it. God!—I've had reason to."

"If you don't believe in Him"—Brown was poking vigorously now—"why bring Him into the conversation?"

Jennings laughed—a short, ugly laugh. "That sounds like you, always putting a fellow in a corner. I use the word, I suppose, to——"

"To give force to what you say? It does it, in a way. But it's not the way you use it when you address Him, is it?"

"I don't address Him." Jennings's tone was defiant.

Brown continued lightly to poke the fire. "About 'that card," said he. "I've often wondered just how many poor chaps it's been responsible for putting down and out."

Jennings stared. "Oh, it's just a joke. I laughed the first time I saw it."

"And the second time?"

"I don't remember. The fellows were all laughing over it when it first came out."

"It *was* a clever thing, a tremendously clever thing, for a man to think of saying. There's so much humour in it. To a man who happened to be already feeling that way, one can see just how it would cheer him up, give him courage, brace him to take a fresh hold."

Jennings grunted. "Oh, well; if you're going to take every joke with such deadly seriousness——"

"You took it lightly, did you? It's seemed like a real joke to you? It's grown funnier and funnier every day, each time it caught your eye?'"

But now Jennings groaned. "No, it hasn't. But that's because it's too true to keep on seeming funny."

Brown suddenly brought his fist down on the arm of Jennings's rocker with a thump which made his nerve-strung visitor jump in his chair. "It *isn't* true! It's not the saying of a brave man, it's the whine of a coward. Brave men don't say that sort of thing. The sort of thing they do say—sometimes to other men, oftener to themselves alone—is what a famous Englishman said: '*If you do fight, fight it out; and don't give in while you can stand and see!*' How's that for a motto? If that had been tacked on the wall in your office all this while, would it have made you feel like giving up, every time you looked at it?"

Brown's eyes were glowing. Jennings had slumped down in his chair, his head on his hand, his face partly hidden from his host. There was silence in the room.

Brown kept Jennings overnight, making a bed for him on his couch, where he could see the fire. As Jennings sat on the couch, ready to turn in, Brown came out from his bedroom, a long figure in his bathrobe and slippers, and knelt down before the old rocking-chair. Jennings, in his surprise, sat perfectly still, looking at him. He could see Brown's lean, strong face in profile, the fine head—it was a very fine head, though perhaps Jennings did not appreciate that—a little lifted, the eyes closed. Brown prayed in a conversational tone, as if the One he addressed were in the room above, with an opening between.

Then he rose, a little tender smile on his face, said, "Good-night, old man," and went away into the inner room—the door of which he did not close.

What did he leave behind him? What was in the air? Was this a common room, a homely room, lighted only by a smoldering fire? What was it which suddenly and unaccountably gripped George Jennings's heart, so that a sob rose in his throat?   What made him want to cry, like a schoolboy, with his head on his arms? With all his long misery, tears had never once come to his relief.   His heart had been hard and his eyes dry.   Now, somehow, he felt something give way.

.   .   .   .   .

Jennings slept all night, and came out to breakfast with a queer, shamefaced aspect, yet with considerably less heaviness of foot than he had shown the night before.   He ate heartily, as well he might, for the food was extremely appetizing.   When he got up to go he stood still by his chair, seeming to be trying to say something.   Seeing this, Brown came over to him and put his hand on his shoulder.

"Yes, lad?" said he interrogatively.   He was smiling and the smile transformed his face, as always.

"I—feel better, this morning," stammered

Jennings. "I—want to thank you. I'm ashamed of the way I talked last night. It was as you said. I knew better, but I couldn't seem to—to——"

Brown nodded. "Of course you knew better," he said heartily. "We all know better. Every man prays—at some time or other. It's when we stop praying that things get dark. Begin again, and something happens. It *always* happens. And sometimes the thing that happens is that we get a good sleep and are able to see things differently in the morning. Goodbye—and come back to-night."

"Shall I?" Jennings asked eagerly.

"Surely. We'll have oysters to-night, roasted on the half-shell over the coals in the fireplace. Like 'em?"

"I never ate any that way," admitted Jennings. "It sounds good." And he smiled broadly, a real smile at last.

"Wait till you try them," promised Brown.

III

BROWN'S BORROWED BABY

On the following Saturday, at five in the afternoon, the previous hours having been filled with a long list of errands of all sorts, yet all having to do with people, and the people's affairs, seldom his own, Brown turned his steps homeward. The steps lagged a little, for he was tired.

At the house next his own—a shabby little house, yet with rows of blooming scarlet geraniums in tin cans on its two lower window sills, and clean, if patched, muslin curtains behind the plants—Brown turned in once more. Standing in the kitchen doorway he put a question:

"Mrs. Kelcey, may I borrow Norah for an hour?"

The person addressed looked up from her work, grinned a broad Irish grin, pushed back a lock of bothersome hair with a soapy hand, and answered heartily:

"To be shure ye may, Misther Brown. I says to mesilf an hour ago, I says, 'Happen he'll come for Nory to-night, it bein' Saturday night, an' him bein' apt to come of a Saturday night.' So I give her her bath early, to get her out o' the way before the bhoys come home. So it's clane she is, if she ain't got into no mischief the half hour."

She dashed into the next room and returned triumphant, her youngest daughter on her arm. Five minutes later Brown bore little Norah Kelcey into his bachelor domain, wrapped in her mother's old plaid shawl, her blue eyes looking expectantly from its folds. It was not the first time she had paid a visit to the place—she remembered what there was in store for her there. She was just two years old, was Norah, a mere slip of an Irish baby, with a tangled mop of dark curls above eyes of deep blue set in bewildering lashes, and with a mouth like a freshly budded rose.

Brown withdrew the shawl and knelt on the floor before her. Bim, who had welcomed the two with eagerness, sat down beside them.

"You see, Bim," explained his master, "I had to have something human to love for an hour or two. You're pretty nearly human, I know, but not quite. Norah is human—she's flesh-and-blood. A fellow gets starved for the touch of flesh-and-blood sometimes, Bim."

He bent over the child. Then he lifted her again and bore her into his bedroom. Clean and wholesome she was without question, but he disliked the faint odour of laundry soap which hung about her. Smiling at her, playing with her, making a game of it, he gently bathed the little face and neck, the plump arms and hands, using a clear toilet soap with a most delicate sugges-

tion of fragrance. When he brought her back
to his fireside she was a small honey-pot for
sweetness and daintiness, and fit for the caresses
she was sure to get.

Brown sat down with her upon his knee. He
had given her a tiny doll to snuggle in her arms,
and she was quiet as a kitten.

"Norah," said he, speaking softly, "you are
adorable. Your eyes are the colour of deep-sea
water and they make havoc with my heart.
That heart, by the way, is soft as melting snow
to-night, Norah. It's longing for all the old
things, longing so hard it aches like a bruise.
It's done its best to be stoical about this exile,
but there are times when stoicism is a failure.
This is one of those times.   Norah baby, would
you mind very much if I kiss the back of your
little neck?"

Norah did not mind in the least.

" All right, little human creature," said Brown,
placing her upon the hearth-rug to play with

Bim's silky brown ears, "you've given me as much comfort as one of us is likely to give another, in a world where everybody starves for something he can't have, and only God knows what the fight for self-denial costs. Shall we have supper now, Norah and Bim? Milk for Norah, bones for Bim, meat for Donald Brown —and a prayer for pluck and patience for us all!"

IV

BROWN'S SISTER SUE

It was a rainy, windy, November night. Brown and Bim were alone together—temporarily. Suddenly, above the howling of the wind sounded sharply the clap of the old knocker on the door. Brown laid down his book—reluctantly, for he was human. A woman's figure, clad from head to foot in furs, sprang from the car at the curb, ran across the sidewalk, and in at the open door.

"Go back to the hotel and come for me at twelve, Simpson," she said to her chauffeur as she passed him, and the next moment she was inside the house and had flung the door heavily shut behind her.

"O Don!" she cried, and assailed the tall figure before her with a furry embrace, which was returned with a right good will.

"Well, well, Sue girl! Have you driven seventy miles to see me?" was Brown's response. Bim, circling madly around the pair, barked his emotion.

"Is this——" began Brown's visitor, glancing rapidly about her as she released herself. "Is this——" she began again, and stopped helplessly. Then, "O Don!" she said once more, and again, "O Don!"—and laughed.

"Yes, I know," said Brown, smiling. "Here, let me take off your furs. It's pretty warm here, I imagine. Bim and I are apt to keep a lot of wood on the fire."

"Bim?"

"At your feet—and your service."

The lady looked at the dog, who stood watching her.

"Your only companion, Don?" she asked.

"My best chum. He's so nearly human he understands at this moment that you don't think him handsome. Never mind! We're used to it, aren't we, Bim? Come over and take this chair, Sue. Are you cold? Would you like something hot? Tea—or coffee?"

She sat in the chair he drew to the fire for her. As he looked at his sister's charming, youthful face, and saw her sitting there in her handsome street dress with its various little indications of wealth and fashion—the gold-meshed purse on its slender chain, the rare jewel in the brooch at the throat, the flashing rings on the white hands —he drew in his breath in an incredulous little whistle.

"Is it really you, Sis?" he said. "You look pretty good to me, do you know, sitting there in my old chair!"

She glanced at the arm of the old rocker, worn smooth by the rubbing of many hands.

"Why do you have such a chair?" she answered impatiently—or so it sounded. "Why in the world, if you must live in a hovel like this, don't you make yourself comfortable? Send home for some easy chairs, and rugs and pictures." Her eye wandered about the room. "And a decent desk—and—and—a well-bred dog!"

He laughed. "A better bred dog, in one sense, than Bim you couldn't find. His manners are finer than those of most men. And as for this being a hovel, you do it injustice. It was built at the beginning of the last century by a titled Englishman, who used it for an office on his estate. Look at the big oak beams. Look at the floor, the doors, the fireplace. It's a distinguished little old house, Sue. Admit it!"

She shook her head. "I'll admit nothing, except that you are the most eccentric fellow who ever lived, to come off here and stay all by yourself, when you've been the idol of a congregation like St. Timothy's—and might still be their idol, if you would take just a little more assistance and not kill yourself with work. I've no patience with you, Don!"

He did not reply to this. Instead, he asked again gently, "Shall it be tea or coffee, Sue?" He stood in the doorway which led to the kitchen and added, as she hesitated, that he could give her an excellent brand of either.

"Coffee, then," she chose, and sat staring into the fire until her brother returned with his earthenware pot and the other essentials for the brewing of coffee, all set forth on a small tray. When, presently, he offered her a fragrant cup, she drank it eagerly.

"That *is* good," she declared. "I didn't know you could cook. When did you learn?"

"On my vacations in the woods. The guides taught me. LaFitte was a wonderful cook—with certain limitations. I've picked up a few other tricks as well. Would you like something to eat?"

"No, thank you."

She had studied him with attention as he knelt before the fire, noting every detail of his appearance. She now put a question which she had reserved.

"Just how well are you now?"

He looked up. "Don't I look well enough to satisfy you?"

"I can't tell. You are frightfully thin——"

"I never was anything else."

"Do you think this sort of thing is doing as much to make you well as Doctor Brainard's prescription of a voyage and stay in the South Seas?"

"Much more."

"You must be dreadfully lonely."

He was sitting, Turk fashion, on the hearthrug before her, his long legs crossed beneath him, his hands clasping his knees. With the firelight playing over his face and touching the thrown-back chestnut locks of his heavy hair with high lights here and there, he looked decidedly boyish. At her suggestion of his probable loneliness he smiled and glanced at Bim.

"Bim," said he, addressing a curled-up mass of rough brown hair from which looked out two watchful brown eyes, and which responded instantly to the name by resolving itself into an approaching dog, "are we ever lonely? Rarely, Sue. As a matter of fact, we have a good many callers, first and last."

"What sort of callers?"

"Neighbours, and friends."

"You are in a horribly poor locality. I noticed as I came through. Do you mean that you encourage these people to come to see you?"

"We use all the drawing powers we have, Bim and I."

"Do you mean to say," said she, bending forward, "that you are conducting a *mission*— here, in this place? When you ought to be just trying to get well? Oh, what would Doctor

Brainard say?" Her tone was full of consternation.

Brown threw back his head and laughed, a big, hearty laugh which did not sound at all like that of an invalid.

"Brainard seems to be your special anxiety," he said. "Send him down to see me. I'll make him some flapjacks. If there's any one who appreciates good cookery it's Brainard."

"Don," said his sister slowly, studying the face before her, "what are you trying to do?"

"Accomplish a little something while I'm marking time."

"You ought to be resting!"

"I am. This is child's play, compared with the parish of St. Timothy's. And it's lots more fun!"

"You're an ascetic!"

"Never. No crusts and water for me—coffee and flapjacks every time."

Once more she bent toward him. "You are an ascetic. To live in this place, and wear—— What are you wearing? Old clothes and a—— What on earth is that scarf pin? A ten-cent piece?"

He put up his hand. "Benson, the little old watchmaker on the corner, gave me that. No, it's not a dime. It pleases him immensely to see me wear it. It's not bad, Sue. Nonsense!"

"It's not good—cheap!"

He sat smiling up at her, while she regarded him in silence for a minute. Then she broke out again:

"Why—*why* do you do it? Haven't you worked hard enough in your great parish, without allowing yourself to spoil this rest you so much need?"

"Sue," said her brother, "the best cure for certain kinds of overwork is merely more work, only of a different sort. I can't be idle and contented. Can you?"

"Idle! I should like to be idle. I'm rushed to death, all the time. It's killing me."

"Dressmakers and hairdressers—and dinners and bridge and the whole routine of your set," said he. "It is indeed a hard life—I wonder you stand it."

"Don't be ironic!"

"I'm not ironic. I realized, long ago, that it's the hardest life in the world—and pays the least."

She flushed. "I have my charities," she reminded him. "I'm not utterly useless. And my clubs—belonging to them is a duty I owe other women. I try to fulfill it."

"But you're not happy."

"Happy! I've forgotten the meaning of the word. To tell the honest truth, Don, I've been feeling for a long while that I didn't care—how soon it ended."

"Poor little sister!"

A crashing blow upon the door startled Mrs. Breckenridge so that she cried out under her breath. Brown went to the door. A furious gust of wind hurled it wide open beneath his hand, but there was no one upon the doorstep. No one? At his feet lay a bundle, from which sounded a wailing cry. He picked it up, looked up and down a vacant street, closed the door, and came back to Sue Breckenridge by the fire.

"I wonder if they chose the bachelor's doorstep by chance or by intention," he said.

"Sue! Don't be that sort of woman — don't let me think it of you!"

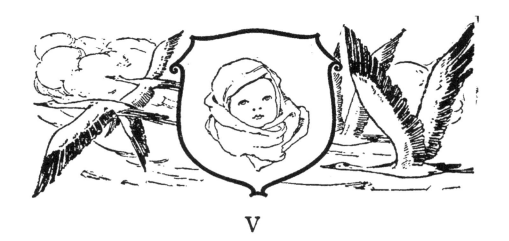

V

BROWN'S UNBORROWED BABY

"Don! Don't take it in! They'll come back for it if you don't—they're watching somewhere. Put it back on the doorstone—don't look at it!"

"Why, Sue!" he answered, and for an instant his eyes flashed reproof into hers. "On such a night?"

"But what can you do with it?"

"Make it comfortable, first."

He was unwrapping the bundle. The child was swathed none too heavily in clean cotton comforters; it was crying frantically, and its hands, as Brown's encountered them in the unwinding, were cold and blue. There emerged from the wrappings an infant of possibly six weeks' existence in a world which had used it ill.

"Will you take him while I get some milk?" asked Brown, as naturally as if handing crying babies over to his sister were an everyday affair with them both.

She shook her head, backing away. "Oh, mercy, no! I shouldn't know what to do with it."

"Sue!" Her brother's tone was suddenly stern. "Don't be that sort of woman—don't let me think it of you!"

He continued to hold out the small wailing bundle. She bit her lip, reluctantly extended unaccustomed arms, and received the foundling into them.

"Sit down close by the fire, my dear, and get those frozen little hands warm. A bit of mothering won't hurt either of you." And Brown strode away into the kitchen with a frown between his brows. He was soon back with a small cupful of warm milk and water, a teaspoon, and a towel.

"Do you expect to feed a tiny baby with a teaspoon?" Sue asked with scorn.

"You don't know much about babies, do you, Sue? Well, I may have some trouble, but it's too late to get any other equipment from my neighbours, and I'll try my luck."

She watched with amazement the proceedings which followed. Brown sat down with the baby cradled on his left arm, tucked the half-unfolded towel beneath its chin, and with the cup conveniently at hand upon the table began to convey the milk, drop by drop, to the little mouth.

"I don't see how you dare do it. You might choke the child to death."

"Not a bit. He'll swallow a lot of atmosphere and it may give him a pain, but that's better than starving. Isn't it, Baby?"

"You act as if you had half a dozen of your

own. What in the world do you know about babies?"

"Enough to puff me up with pride. Mrs. Murdison, my right-hand neighbour, is the mother of five; Mrs. Kelcey, on my left, has six —and two of them are twins. One twin was desperately ill a while ago. I became well acquainted with it—and with the other five."

"Don!" Again his sister gazed at him as if she found him past comprehension. "You— *you!* What would your friends—our friends— say, if they knew?"

Putting down the teaspoon and withdrawing the towel, Brown snuggled the baby in his left arm. Warmth and food had begun their work in soothing the little creature, and it was quiet, its eyelids drooping heavily.

He got up, carried the baby to the couch, with one hand arranged a steamer rug lying there so that it made a warm nest, and laid the small bundle in it.

Then he returned to his chair by the fire.   He lifted his eyes for a long, keen look into his sister's face, until she stirred restlessly under the inspection.

"Well, what do you see?" she asked.

"I see," said Brown slowly, "a woman who is trying to live without remembering her immortality."

She shivered suddenly, there before the blazing fire.   "I'm not sure that I believe in it," she said fiercely.   "Now I've shocked you, Don, but I can't help it.   I'm not sure of anything, these days.   That's why——"

"Why you want to forget.   But you can't forget.   And the reason why you can't forget is because you do believe in it.   Every day people are trying to forget one of the greatest facts in the universe.   They may deny it with their lips, but with their hearts they know it is true."

She did not answer.   Her brother drew his chair closer, leaned forward, and took one of the

jewelled hands in his.　He spoke very gently, and
in his voice was a certain quality of persuasion
which belongs not to all voices which would per-
suade.

"Sue, make room in your life for a little child.
You need him."

Her glance evaded his, flashed past his to the
small, still bundle on the couch.　Then, suddenly, into her unhappy eyes leaped a suspicion.
She straightened in her chair.

"You don't mean—you're not suggesting——"

He smiled, comprehending.　"No, no—nothing like that.　Your heart isn't big enough for
that—yet.　It's the mothers of children who
make room for the waifs, or those who have long
been mothers in heart and have been denied.　You don't belong to either of those
classes, do you?"

She drew a stifled breath.　"You don't know
what you are talking about, Don.　How could
you, a bachelor like you?"

"Couldn't I? Well, Sue, if fathers may be divided into the same two classes, I might be found in one of them."

She stared at him. "You? Oh, I can't believe it. You could have married long ago, if you had wanted to. You could have married anybody—simply anybody!"

"You do me too much honour—or discredit, I'm not just sure which."

"But it's true. With your position—and your money! Rich and brilliant clergymen aren't so common, Donald Brown. And your personality, your magnetism! Men care for you. Women have always hung on your words!"

He made a gesture of distaste; got up.

"Sterility of soul is a worse thing than sterility of body," said he. "But sometimes—God cures the one when He cures the other."

"But you never prescribed this strange thing before."

He smiled. "I've been learning some things

out here, Sue, that I never learned before. One of them is how near God is to a little child."

"You've learned that—of your neighbours?" Her accent was indescribable.

"Of my neighbours—and friends."

It was time for her to go. He helped her into her great fur coat and himself fastened it in place. When she was ready she turned from the window from which she had tried in vain to see her surroundings, and threw at her brother a question which seemed to take him unawares.

"Don, do you know anything about Helena these days?"

Though his face did not change, something about him suggested the mental bracing of himself for a shock. He shook his head.

"She's dropped everything she used to care for. Nobody knows why. Her mother's in despair about her—you know what a society leader Mrs. Forrest has always been. She can't understand Helena—nor can anybody."

"She's not ill?"

"Apparently not; she's as wonderful to look at as ever, when one meets her—which one seldom does. The girls say she walks miles every day, so she must be well in body, though even that doesn't assure Mrs. Forrest. I thought, possibly, you might know. You and Helena used to be such friends."

"We are still, I hope."

His sister's eyes were not easily to be deceived, and they were positive they saw pain in the eyes which met her own.

"Don," she said softly, "may I ask you one question?"

"Please don't."

"When you were a little boy, and you got hurt in any way, you used to run away and hide. Are you—hiding now?"

His eyes grew dark with sudden anger, but he replied with self-control:

"You will have to think what you like about

that, Sue. If that is the way the thing looks to you—so be it!"

The sound of the returning car made Mrs. Breckenridge speak hurriedly:

"I didn't mean to be unkind, Don boy. Nobody knows better than I that you are no coward. Only—only—you know an ascetic denies himself things that he needn't. And— you *are* an ascetic!"

"Can I never convince you of your mistake about that?" he answered; and now his lips smiled again, a little stiffly.

She embraced him once more, stopped to say beseechingly, "You won't keep that baby here, will you, Don?" and, receiving his assurance that he would consult with his neighbours in the morning as to the welfare of the foundling, took her departure.

Left alone Brown went back into the quiet room. The baby was stirring among its wrappings. Bim, who had roused himself to see the visitor off, came and poked his nose into the bundle.

"We never know what's coming, Bim, do we?" asked Brown of his companion. "Sometimes it's what we want, and sometimes not. But—if we are to teach others we must be taught ourselves, Bim. And that's what's happening now."

VI

BROWN'S PERSISTENT MEMORY

"I wonder," he said to himself an hour later, "if it's any use to go to bed at all!"

He was walking the floor with the baby in his arms. Bim, puzzled and anxious, walked by his side, looking up at the small bundle with a glance which seemed to say, "What in the world are we going to do with it?"

Whether the feeding from the teaspoon had disagreed with its digestion could not be discovered, but clearly the baby was unhappy. It was quiet when walked with but upon being put down immediately set up such an outcry that the bachelor, unaccustomed, could not listen to it with stoicism. Therefore, when he had endured the sound as long as he could, he had taken the little visitor up and was now walking with it, himself in bathgown and slippers.

"It may be a pin, Bim," said he suddenly.

He sat down before the fire, laid the baby upon its face on his knees and began cautiously to investigate. He loosened the tiny garments one by one, until he had reached the little body and could assure himself that no sharp point was responsible for the baby's discomfort. He gently rubbed the small back, wondering, as he did so, at the insignificant area his hand nearly covered. Under this treatment the wailing gradually quieted.

"Bim," said he resignedly, "we shall have to sit up with him—for a while, at least."

Bim walked over to the window.

"No," said his master, "we can't disturb our neighbours at this time of night. We must see it through. If we can manage to read, it will make the time go faster."

He reached for a book, opened it at a mark, and began to read, his hand, meanwhile, steadily maintaining the soothing motion up and down the baby's back. But his thoughts were not upon the page. Instead, they took hold upon one phrase his sister had used—one phrase, which had brought up to him a certain face as vividly as the sudden presentation of a portrait might have done.

"She's as wonderful to look at as ever."

Was she? Well, she had been wonderful to look at—there could be no question of that. He had looked at her, and looked, and looked again, until his eyes had blurred with the dazzle of the vision. And having looked, there could be no possible forgetting, no merciful blotting out of the recollection of that face. He had tried to forget it, to forget the whole absorbing personality, had tried with all his strength, but the thing could not be done. It seemed to him sometimes that the very effort to efface that image only cut its outlines deeper into his memory.

The baby began to cry afresh, with sudden, sharp insistence. Brown took it up and strode the floor with it again.

"Poor little chap!" he murmured. "You can't have what you want, and I can't have what I want. But it doesn't do a bit of good to cry about it—eh?"

The knocker sounded. Bim growled.

"At this hour!" thought Brown, with a glance at his watch lying on the table. It was nearly two in the morning.

Holding the baby in the crook of his arm he crossed the floor and opened the door gingerly, sheltering the baby behind it.

"Is it the toothache, Misther Brown?" inquired an eagerly pitiful voice. "Or warse?"

Mrs. Kelcey came in, her shawl covering her unbound hair—his next-door neighbour and little Norah's mother. Her face was full of astonishment at sight of Brown in his bathgown and the baby in his arms.

"I'm mighty glad to see you," Brown assured her. "I don't know what to do with him, poor little fellow. I think it must be a pain."

"The saints and ahl!" said Mrs. Kelcey. She took the baby from him with wonted, motherly arms. "The teeny thing!" she exclaimed. "Where——"

"Left on my doorstep."

"An' ye thried to get through the night with him! Why didn't ye bring him to me at wanst?"

"It was late—your lights were out. How did you know I was up?"

"Yer lights wasn't out. I was up with me man—Pat's a sore fut, an' I was bathin' it to quiet him. I seen yer lights. Ye sit up till ahl hours, I know, but I cud see the shadow movin' up and down. I says to Pat, 'He's the toothache, maybe, and me with plinty of rimidies nixt door.'"

She turned her attention to the tiny creature in her lap.   She inquired into the case closely, and learned how the child had been fed with a teaspoon.

"To think of a single man so handy!" she exclaimed admiringly.   "But maybe he shwallied a bit too much air with the feedin'."

"He swallowed all the air there was at hand," admitted Brown, "and precious little milk. But he seemed hungry, and I thought he was too little to go all night without being fed."

"Right ye were, an' 'tis feedin' he nades agin —only not with a shpoon. I'll take him home an' fix up a bit of a bottle for him, the poor thing. An' I'll take him at wanst, an' let ye get to bed, where ye belong, by the looks of ye."

"You're an angel, Mrs. Kelcey. I hate to let you take him, with all you have on your hands——"

"Shure, 'tis the hands that's full that can always hold a bit more.   An' a single man can't be bothered with cast-off childher, no matter how big his heart is, as we well know."

And Mrs. Kelcey departed, with the baby under her shawl and a motherly look for the man who opened the door for her and stood smiling at her in the lamplight as she went away.

But when he had thrown himself, at last, on his bed, wearily longing for rest, he found he had still to wrestle a while with the persistent image of the face which was "wonderful to look at," before kindly slumber would efface it with the gray mists of oblivion.

VII

BROWN'S FINANCIAL RESOURCES

"There, Tom, how's that? Does it droop as much as the one on the other side?"

Tom Kelcey, aged fourteen, squinted critically at the long festoon of ground-pine between the centre of the chimney-breast and the angle of the dingy old oak-beamed ceiling.

"Drop her a couple of inches, Misther Brown," he suggested. "No, not so much. There, that's the shtuff. Now you've got her, foine and dandy."

Brown stepped down from the chair on which he had been standing, and stood off with Tom to view the effect.

"Yes, that's exactly right," said he, "thanks

to your good eye. The room looks pretty well, eh? Quite like having a dinner party."

"It's ilegant, Misther Brown, that's what it is," said a voice in the doorway behind them. "Tom bhoy, be afther takin' the chair back to the kitchen for him."

Mrs. Kelcey, mother of Tom, and next-door neighbour to Brown, advanced into the room. She was laden with a big basket, which Brown, perceiving, immediately took from her.

"Set it down careful, man," said she. "The crust on thim pies is that delicate it won't bear joltin'. I had the saints' own luck with 'em this toime, praise be."

"That's great," said Brown. "But I haven't worried about that. You never have anything else, I'm sure."

Mrs. Kelcey shook her head in delighted protest.

"The table is jist the handsomest I iver laid

eyes on," she asserted, modestly changing the subject.

"It is pretty nice, isn't it?" agreed Brown warmly, surveying the table with mixed emotions. When he stopped to think of what Mrs. Hugh Breckenridge would say at sight of that table, set for the Thanksgiving dinner her brother, Donald Brown, was giving that afternoon, he experienced a peculiar sensation in the region of his throat. He was possessed of a vivid sense of humour which at times embarrassed him sorely. If it had not been that his bigness of heart kept his love of fun in order he would have had great difficulty, now and then, in comporting himself with necessary gravity.

Mrs. Kelcey herself had arranged that table, spending almost the entire preceding day in dashing about the neighbourhood, borrowing from Brown's neighbours the requisite articles. Brown's own stock of blue-and-white ware proving entirely inadequate, besides being in Mrs.

Kelcey's eyes by no means fine enough for the occasion, she had unhesitatingly requisitioned every piece of china she could lay hands on in the neighbourhood. She had had no difficulty whatever in borrowing more than enough, for every woman in the block who knew Brown was eager to lend her best. The result was such an array of brilliantly flowered plates and cups and dishes of every style and shape, that one's gaze, once riveted thereon, could with difficulty be removed.

When Brown had first conceived this festival it had been with the idea of sending to the nearest city for a full equipment, if an inexpensive one, of all the china and glass, linen and silver necessary for the serving of the meal. But upon thinking it over it occurred to him that such an outlay would not only arouse his new friends' suspicion of his financial resources, it would deprive them of one of the chief joys in such a neighbourhood as this in which he was abiding—

that of the personal sharing in the details of the dinner's preparation and the proud lending of their best in friendly rivalry.

Therefore the table, as it now stood before him in all but complete readiness for the feast, bore such witness to the warmth of esteem in which the neighbourhood held him, not to mention its resourcefulness in fitting together adjuncts not originally intended for partnership, as must have touched the heart of a dinner-giver less comprehending than Donald Brown, late of St. Timothy's great and prosperous parish

To begin with, the table itself had been set up in its place in the front room by Tim Lukens the carpenter, who when he was sober was one of the cleverest of artisans. Starting with two pairs of sawhorses and continuing with smooth pine boards, he had constructed a table of goodly proportions and of a solidity calculated to withstand successfully the demand likely to be made upon it. Over this table-top Mrs. Kelcey had laid—without thought, it must be admitted, of any intermediary padding such as certain mistaken hostesses consider essential—three freshly and painstakingly laundered tablecloths, her own, Mrs. Murdison's, and Mrs. Lukens's best, cunningly united by stitches hardly discoverable except by a too-searching eye.

The foundations thus laid, the setting of the table had been a delightful task for Mrs. Kelcey, assisted as she was by Mrs. Murdison, who frequently differed from her in points of arrangement but who yielded most of them upon hearing, as she frequently did, Mrs. Kelcey's verbal badge of office: "Misther Brown put me in charrge, Missus Murdison. He says to me, he says, 'Missus Kelcey, do jist as ye think best.'" Together the two had achieved a triumph, and the table now stood forth glowingly ready for its sixteen guests, from the splendid bunch of scarlet geraniums in an immense pink and blue bowl with an Indian's head on one side, to the sixteen

chairs, no two exactly alike, which had been ob-
tained from half as many houses.

As for the dinner itself, there was no patch-
work about that. Brown himself had supplied
the essentials, trusting that the most of his
guests could have no notion whatever of the
excessively high cost of turkeys that season, or of
the price of the especial quality of butter and
eggs which he handed over to Mrs. Kelcey to be
used in the preparation of the dishes which he
and she had decided upon. That lady, however,
had had some compunctions as she saw the un-
stinted array of materials an astonished grocer's
boy had delivered upon her kitchen table two
days before the dinner, and had expressed herself to Mrs. Murdison as concerned lest Mr.
Brown had spent more than he could well
afford.

"'Tis the big hearrt of him that leads his
judgment asthray," she said, exulting none the
less, as she spoke, over the prospect of handling

all those rich materials and for once having the chance to display her skilled cookery. "I said as much as I dared, lest I hurrt his pride, but—''Tis but wanct a year, Missus Kelcey,' says he, an' I said no more."

The thrifty Scotswoman shook her head. "The mon kens nae mair aboot the cost o' things than a cheild," said she. "But 'twould be, as ye say, a peety to mak' him feel we dinna appreciate his thocht o' us.'"

So they had done their best for him, and the result was a wonderful thing. To his supplies they had surreptitiously added small delicacies of their own. Mrs. Kelcey contributed a dish of fat pickles, luscious to the eye and cooling to the palate. Mrs. Murdison brought a jar of marmalade of her own making—a rare delicacy, though the oranges were purchased of an Italian vender who had sold out an over-ripe stock at a pittance. Mrs. Lukens supplied a plate of fat doughnuts, and Mrs. Burke sent over a big platter of molasses candy. Thus the people of the neighbourhood had come to feel the affair one to which not only had they been bidden, but in which they were all in a way entertainers.

The boys of the district, also, had their share in the fun. Though not invited to the dinner proper, they had been given a hint that if they dropped in that evening after their fathers and mothers had departed there might be something left—and what boys would not rather "drop in" after that fashion, by the back door, than go decorously in at the front one? So they had been eager to furnish decorations for the party, according to Brown's suggestion, by going in a body to the woods three miles away and bringing back a lavish supply of ground-pine. They had spent two happy evenings helping Brown make this material into ropes, while he told them stories, and there was not a boy of them all who would not cheerfully have lent his shoulders to the support of the dinner-table throughout the coming meal, if it had suddenly been reported that Tim Lukens's sawhorses were untrustworthy.

"Now, Misther Brown, I'll be goin' home to see to the twins and get me man to dhress himsilf, an' thin I'll be back. Have no fear—av'rythin's doin' foine, an' the turrkey's an ilegant brown jist beginnin' to show. If I'm not back in tin minutes ye moight baste him wanct, but have no other care."

"I'll be delighted to baste him, thank you," Brown responded. "And I have no cares at all, with you in charge. I only hope you won't be too tired to enjoy the dinner. You've been busy every minute since dawn."

"Shure, 'tis the labour of love makes the worrk aisy," she responded, and then, attacked by a sudden and most unusual wave of shyness, disappeared out of the door.

Brown, standing with his back to the fire,

smiled to himself. Well he knew that since the suffering three-year-old twin son of the Kelceys had spent the night in his pitiful arms and in the morning taken a turn for the better, the entire Kelcey family would have made martyrs of themselves for his sake. It was quite true that that sort of thing, as his sister, Mrs. Breckenridge, had intimated, was not precisely in accordance with the prescription of Dr. Bruce Brainard, distinguished specialist. But if that night had been his last, Donald Brown could not have spent it in a way more calculated to give him pleasure as he closed his eyes. Surely, since life was still his, the love of the Kelceys was not to be despised.

As he dressed for the dinner Brown considered his attire carefully. He could not venture to wear anything calculated to outshine the apparel of his guests, and yet to don the elbow-worn, shiny-backed blue serge of his everyday apparel seemed not to do them quite honour enough. He had not many clothes with him, but he had brought one suit of rough homespun, smart indeed from the viewpoint of the expensive tailor who had made it, but deceivingly unconventional to the eye of the uninitiated. This he put on, taking particular pains to select a very plain cravat, and to fasten in it with care the scarf-pin bestowed upon him by old Benson, the little watchmaker on the corner below. Through the buttonhole in the lapel of his coat he drew a spicy-smelling sprig of ground-pine, chanting whimsically as he did so a couplet from Ben Jonson:

> "Still to be neat, still to be drest,
> As you were going to a feast."

VIII

BROWN'S BIDDEN GUESTS

And now, promptly on the stroke of two, the dinner guests arrived, not a man or woman of them later than five minutes after. Even Mrs. Kelcey, though she had rushed into the kitchen two minutes earlier by the back door, now entered formally with Patrick, her husband, by the front, and only the high flush on her cheek and the sparkle in her blue-black eye told of a sense of her responsibilities.

The company had put on its best for the occasion, there could be no possible question of that. From the pink geranium in Mrs. Kelcey's hair just behind her ear, to the high polish of her husband's boots, the Kelceys were brave and fine. Mrs. Murdison, though soberly gowned in slate-coloured worsted, wore a white muslin kerchief which gave her the air of a plump and comfortable Mother Superior. Mr. Murdison, the only gentleman present who possessed a "suit of blacks," as he himself was accustomed to call it, came in looking like the Scottish preacher whose grandson he was, and lent much dignity to the occasion merely by his presence.

There was a predominance of exquisitely ironed white "shirtwaists" among the costumes of the women, but as these were helped out by much elaborate and dressy neckwear of lace and ribbon the general effect was unquestionably festive. The men were variously attired as to clothing, but every collar was immaculate— most of them had a dazzlingly brilliant finish— and the neckties worn were so varied as to give the eye relief from possible monotony.

In spite of Brown's genial greetings to his guests—he had a special welcoming word for

He was presently fiddling away, while the company sat about, completely
relaxed in spirit

every one—just at first there was a bit of stiff-
ness. The men showed the customary tendency
to support one another through the social ordeal
by standing in a solid group in a corner of the
room, hands behind their backs and an air of
great gravity upon their faces, while they spoke,
if at all, in low and solemn tones. The women, on
the other hand, as ever, did their best to show
themselves entirely at ease by addressing, one
after another, remarks to their host calculated
to prevent his having any doubt as to the sort of
weather now prevailing outside or likely to pre-
vail during the days to come.

Brown, having anticipated this period of
gloom before the feast should actually begin,
had arranged with Mrs. Kelcey that as soon as
the last guest had arrived the company should
sit down at the table. Mrs. Kelcey, true to her
word, gave him the nod without the delay of
more than a minute or two, and promptly the
company seated itself. Brown, drawing back

her chair for Mrs. Murdison, who as his most impressive guest he had placed upon his right, noticed, without seeming to notice, that the little watchmaker did the same for his wife, and with an effect of habit. Speaking of wives, the company being left to seat themselves according to their own notion (Brown having considered the question of dinner cards and discarded it), every man sat down beside his own wife, in some instances being surreptitiously jerked into position by a careful conjugal hand.

Brown, looking about his table with a smile, bent his head. Every eye fell and every ear listened to the words which followed:

"Our Father, we are here in company with Thee and in warm friendliness with one another. We are thankful on this day that we are busy men and women, able to do our work and to be useful in Thy world. Teach us to find in life the joy of living it to please Thee. Amen."

It was Mrs. Kelcey who broke the hush which

followed, by starting from her place to run out into the kitchen and bring on the dinner. From this moment the peculiar fitness of Donald Brown for the duties of host showed itself. That his dinner should be stiff and solemn was not in his intention, if the informality of his own conduct could prevent it. He therefore jumped up from his own place to follow Mrs. Kelcey to the kitchen and bring in the great platter for her, bearing the turkey in a garland of celery leaves, a miracle of luscious-looking brownness.

He had considered the feasibility of serving at least one preliminary course, not so much because it seemed to him impossible to plunge at once into the heartiness of fowl and stuffing as because he wanted to prolong the hour of dining for his guests. But Mrs. Kelcey had promptly vetoed this notion.

"Man, dear," she had said earnestly, "an' why would ye be shpoiling the appetoites of yer company with soup? 'Tis soup they know only too well—but the turrkey! 'Tis manny a long year since Mrs. Murdison and Andy have tasted the loike of it, an' the same with the ithers.   If 'twas chickun, I'll warrant now—we're all glad to make a bit of chickun go furrther with other things—but a grreat turrkey like this wan—— Give it to thim sthrait, Misther Brown, an' that's my advoice.   Ye can take it or lave it."

Brown had accepted this wise counsel, of course, and now saw the full wisdom of it as he beheld the looks of veiled but hungry—one might almost have said starving—anticipation which fell upon the big turkey as it was borne to its place at the end of the table.

"I don't know how an old bachelor is going to make out to carve before such a company," Brown said gaily, brandishing his carving knife. (This was a bit of play-making, for he was a famous carver, having been something of an epicure in days but one year past, and accustomed to demand and receive careful service in his bachelor establishment.) "I wonder if I can manage it. Mr. Benson"—he addressed the old watchmaker—"what do you say to taking my place and helping me out? I'd hate to ruin the bird."

"I say I'll not do it, Mr. Brown," responded old Benson. "Watch-making is my business, and it's watch I'll make now of your carving."

This brave attempt at a witticism brought a fine response, Brown's hearty laugh leading off. And now the ice began to be broken into smaller and smaller bits. Brown's gay spirits, his mirth-provoking observations as he carved the tender fowl, the way in which he appreciated the efforts of his guests to do their part, led them all to forget themselves in greater or less degree. When it came to the actual attacking of the piled-up plates before them, it is true that there ensued considerable significant silence, but it was the silence of approval and enjoyment, not that of failure to be entertained.

If it occurred to Brown to wish himself at some more exalted festival-making with more congenial associates on this Thanksgiving Day, no one would have dreamed it.   To all appearances he was with his best friends, and if he did not partake of the toothsome meal before him with such avidity as they, it would have needed a more discerning person to have recognized it than any one who sat at his board—at his boards, it might be put, remembering Tim Lukens's achievement with the sawhorses.

Tim, himself, was present, sober and subdued but happy.   How it came about that he had not drunk a drop for several weeks, none but Brown and Mrs. Lukens could have told.   Tim's glance was often upon Brown's face—the look in his eyes, now and then, reminded Brown of that in the eyes of his dog Bim when he had earned his master's approval, shy but adoring.

In spite of all there was to eat in that mighty first course of turkey and stuffing and mashed

white potatoes and sirup-browned sweet potatoes, and every possible accompaniment of
gravy and vegetable and relish, not to mention
such coffee as none of them had ever drunk, it
all disappeared with astonishing rapidity down
the throats of the guests. How, indeed, can one
mince and play with his food when he and his
wife have not in their lives tasted so many good
things all at once, and when both have been prepared for the feast by many weeks and months—
and years—of living upon boiled potatoes with a
bit of salt pork, or even upon bread and molasses,
when times were hard? Brown's neighbours
were not of the very poorest, by any means,
but all were thriftily accustomed to self-denial,
and there is no flavour to any dainty like that of
having seldom tasted but of having longed for it
all one's life.

When the second course had come and gone—
it was composed entirely of pies, but of such
pies!—Brown surprised Mrs. Kelcey by going to

a cupboard and bringing out a final treat un-suspected by her. A great basket of fruit, oranges and bananas and grapes, flanked by a big bowl of nuts cunningly set with clusters of raisins, made them all exclaim. Happily, they had reached the exclaiming stage, no longer afraid of their host or of one another.

"It's reckless with his money he is, Patsy," whispered Mrs. Kelcey to her husband. "It'll take a power of it to pay for all o' thim, an' fruit so dear."

"Whist, he knows what he's about," returned Patrick Kelcey, uninclined to remonstrate with any man for giving him that unaccustomed and delightful feeling that his vest buttons must be surreptitiously unloosed or he would burst them off. He helped himself lavishly as he spoke.

By and by, when all had regretfully declined so much as another raisin—"Now we must have some music!" cried Brown. "Tim, did you bring your fiddle?"

Tim Lukens nodded. Carpentry was Tim's vocation, but fiddling was his avocation and dear delight. He was presently fiddling away, while the company sat about, completely relaxed in spirit, and Mrs. Kelcey and Mrs. Murdison hustled the table clear of dishes, refusing sternly Brown's eager offer to help them. And now came the best time of all. Tim played all the old tunes, and when he struck into "Kate Kearney" the company was electrified to hear a rich and vibrant voice take up the words of the song and sing them through to the end.

Sitting carelessly on his pine-bottomed chair —it was one from the Kelcey house—one hand in his pocket, his heavy hair tossed back and his lips smiling, Brown's splendid tones rang through the room and held his listeners enthralled. Never had they heard singing like that. They could have no possible notion of the quality of the voice to which they listened, but they enjoyed its music so thoroughly that the moment the song was ended they were eager for another.   So he sang them another and still another, while the warm blood rolled in under his dark skin, enriching his thin cheek till it looked no longer thin.   He was giving himself up to the task of pleasing his friends, with thorough enjoyment of his own.   After "Kate Kearney" he sang "Annie Laurie," making Andy Murdison's warm Scottish heart under his stiff Scottish manner beat throbbingly in sympathy.   So the hours passed, it never occurring to the company to go home as long as it was having the time of its life, until the sudden discovery of a row of boys' faces peering eagerly in from the darkness of the late afternoon reminded Mrs. Kelcey that she had a family at home.

"The saints be prraised, 'tis afther darrk," said she, rising precipitately, "and the bhoys promised the lavin's of the table!"

They all followed her, suddenly grown shy again as they murmured their thanks.   Their host's cheery parting words eased them over this ordeal, however, and each one left with the comfortable feeling that he had said the right thing.

Two minutes later the house was again invaded, this time by those who felt entirely at home there. With a whoop of joy the boys of the neighbourhood took possession, and as they did so a curious thing happened: Donald Brown himself became a boy among them.

But this was not the only curious thing which happened.

The sixteen guests at the dinner, in spite of the generous supplies, had not left many "lavin's." The great turkey had little remaining now upon his bones and nothing at all inside of him; the potatoes and vegetables had been entirely consumed; of the pies there remained a solitary wedge. But Brown, smiling broadly, attended to these difficulties. He had the air of a commissary who knew of unlimited supplies.

"Tom," he commanded, "pick three boys and

go down cellar with them, and into the little storeroom at the right."

Tom, grinning, made a lightning-like selection of assistants, and dove down the steep and narrow stairway from the kitchen.

"Burke and Jimpsey, explore the cupboard opening from my bedroom, and bring out whatever you find there that looks good to eat."

Before the words were out of his mouth Burke and Jimpsey had disappeared.

"Tub and Jiggers, look under my bed, and haul out a long box you'll find there."

The two fell over each other to do his bidding. In less time than it takes to tell it, the emissaries were returning with their spoils. A whole cooked turkey, only slightly inferior in size to the original one, appeared to the accompaniment of howls of joy. It was cold, to be sure, but what boy would mind that—and to the critical palate is not cold turkey even more delicious than hot? There were piles and piles of sandwiches with the most delectable filling, there were pies and more pies, and there were fruit and cake and candy. Brown had not feared lest these later guests suspect him of too long a purse; he had ordered without stint, and his orders had been filled by a distant firm of caterers and sent by express.

Now there were girls in the neighbourhood as well as boys. By a mysterious invitation they had been summoned to the home of one of their number, a small cripple, and were there at the very moment rejoicing in all manner of festivities. Nobody knew how it had happened, nor where the good things came from, except the little girl who was their hostess, and wild horses could not have dragged the wonderful secret from her. Brown himself, making merry with his boys, remembered the girls with a comfortable feeling at his heart that for once, at least, a goodly number of people, young and old, were happier than they had ever been before in their lives on Thanksgiving Day.

As for his own immediate entertaining the
revel now began—no lesser word describes it.
If, before the departure of his dinner guests,
Brown had experienced a slight feeling of fatigue,
it disappeared with the pleasure of seeing
his present company disport themselves. They
were not in the least afraid of him—how should
they be, when he had spent months in the win-
ning of their confidence and affection by every
clever wile known to the genuine boy lover?
That they respected him was plainly shown by
the fact that, ill trained at home as most of them
had been, with him they never overstepped certain bounds. At the lifting of a finger he could
command their attention, though the moment
before their boisterousness had known no limits.

If the earlier guests had been surprisingly
rapid in their consumption of the dinner, these
later ones were startlingly so. Like grain before a flock of hungry birds, like ice beneath a
bonfire, the viands, lavishly provided though

they had been, melted away in almost the twinkling of an eye.   And it was precisely as the last enormous mouthful of cherry pie vanished down Jiggers Quigg's happy throat that the unexpected happened.

IX

BROWN'S UNBIDDEN GUESTS

The front door, opening directly into the living-room, with its long table, and its flashing fire lighting the eager faces round it—nobody had thought of or bothered to make any other light in that room—was flung open by a fur-gloved hand, and a large figure appeared in the doorway. A ruddy face looked in upon the scene. This face possessed a pair of keen gray eyes, a distinguished nose, and a determined mouth beneath a close-trimmed moustache with flecks of gray in it.

Brown sprang up. "Doctor Brainard!" he cried joyfully, and came forward with outstretched hand.

"Then forgive me," said he, laying light but determined hold
upon her veil

The unexpected guest advanced. Behind him appeared others. To the dazed and gazing boys these people might have come from Greenland, so enveloped were they in defences against the cold. Motor coats of rich fur, furry hats and caps, floating silken veils, muffs, rugs—wherever they came from they could not have minded coming, sharp as was the November air outside, as the boys, who had been hanging about the the house since the first approach of twilight, well knew.

Dr. Bruce Brainard was followed by two men and three women. In the flickering firelight Brown was obliged to come close to each, as in smiling silence they approached him, before he could make sure whom the furs and scarfs enshrouded.

"Sue!" he exclaimed, discovering his sister. "And Hugh Breckenridge! This is great, brother-in-law! Mrs. Brainard—can it be Mrs. Brainard? How kind of you! You must have known how I've been wanting to see you. Webb Atchison, is that you, looming behind there? How are you, old fellow? But—this lady in the veil——"

He bent closer as he took the gloved hand outstretched, but all he could make out in the traitorous light was a pair of dark eyes, and lips that must be laughing behind the heavy silken veil.

"Do I know her?" he asked, looking round upon the others, who were watching him.

"You have met her," Hugh Breckenridge assured him.

"Several times," added Webb Atchison.

"But not of late," said Brown, "or else I——"

"Once to have seen her," declared Doctor Brainard, "means never to forget."

"You put me in a hard place," Brown objected, trying in vain to distinguish outlines through the veil. "She isn't going to lift it? Must I guess?"

"Of course you must guess, Don," cried his sister.

"How can he?" laughed Breckenridge. "He knows so many fair beings of about that height, and furs and veils are disguising things. Without them, of course, though she wore a mask, he would have no difficulty."

"Will you speak one word?" asked Brown of the unknown.

She shook her head.

"Then—forgive me, but I'm puzzled," said he, laying light but determined hold upon the veil. "I can't imagine at all who—would honour me——"

He gently lifted the veil. The others saw his expression change as the drawn folds revealed a face whose dark-eyed beauty was vividly enhanced by the fire-glow upon cheeks which the November frost had stung into a wonder colour. There was a general laugh of appreciation.

"Never would have thought it, eh?" chuckled

Webb Atchison, a fine and prosperous figure of a bachelor past his first youth but not yet arrived at middle age, and with the look of one who does what he pleases with other people. "Well, it wasn't her plan, I assure you. She was horror-stricken when she learned where we were bound."

"Donald Brown in his bachelor apartment in the Worthington was one person, this queer fellow living in a roadside cabin is quite another," suggested Dr. Bruce Brainard quizzically. "Still, I'll warrant Miss Forrest will confess to a bit of curiosity, when she found she was in for it."

"Were you curious?" asked Donald Brown. He was still looking steadily down into the lifted face of the person before him. Into his own face had come a look as of one who has been taken unawares at a vulnerable point, but who has instantly rallied his forces to stand out the attack.

"They were all curious," answered Miss Forrest, and the sound of her voice was different from that of the other voices. If, as Doctor

Brainard had jestingly but truthfully said, one who had seen her would not forget her, a similar statement might with equal truth be made of the hearing of her voice.   The one word Brown had asked from her lips could certainly have revealed her to him—and would have done so while he had a memory.

"To see if we know how to keep Thanksgiving here?" Brown inquired of the group, though his eyes came back again to Helena Forrest's face.

"To see if you had anything to be thankful for," cried Sue Breckenridge.   "Well, Don, now that we are here, are you going to invite us to stay?   Or—is your present company——"

Brown wheeled and went over to the boys, who were staring, open-eyed and motionless.

"You'll help me out, fellows, won't you?" he said in a low tone—and they felt him still one of them, for the tone was the old one of comradeship.   "You see, I have nowhere to ask my guests to sit down.   If each of you will take what you can at a time, and carry everything out into the kitchen, and then take out the table, I'll be much obliged. You are coming again soon, you know; but for to-night, you see, I must call it off. Tom, you'll see to taking off the tablecloth, will you? Fold it up any sort of way, but don't let the crumbs get out. All right?"

There was a tumultuous pushing back of chairs. In short order it was all accomplished. The guests stood at one side, looking at the boys as curiously as the boys had looked at them, while the dishes disappeared as fast as many hands could carry them. The big bowl of geraniums was removed by Brown himself, who set it carefully upon his reading-table at the side of the room, and the tablecloth was painstakingly manipulated by Tom Kelcey so that hardly a crumb fell upon the floor. There was one crash of crockery in the kitchen, followed by a smothered howl from the boy who in his agitation had done the deed, but this was the only accident.

Brown turned again to his guests.

"Now," said he, "will you make yourselves at home?   It's a cold night out.   Let's have off the furs and sit by the fire.   Mrs. Brainard, allow me to help you out of that coat.   This is the happiest sort of a surprise for me!"

X

BROWN'S ANSWERS TO QUESTIONS

Donald Brown stood at the end of his hearth, his elbow resting on the chimney-piece, his eyes, narrowed a little between the lashes, intently regarding these latest guests of his. He was in the shadow, they were in the strong light of the fire. A great lump of cannel coal, recently laid upon the red-hot embers and half-burned logs of the afternoon fire, had just broken apart with a great hissing and crackling of the pitchy richness of its inner formation, and the resultant glow of rosy light which enveloped the figures before the hearth, against the duller background of the room, otherwise unillumined, made them stand out like figures in a cleverly lighted tableau.

They were much more interesting to Brown, however, than anything he had ever seen in the set and artificial radiance of the calcium light. He knew well every face there, and yet, after his year's exile and in contrast to the faces at which he had been lately looking, they formed a more engrossing study than any he had known for many months.

In the centre of the circle, in Brown's old red-cushioned rocker and most comfortable chair, sat Mrs. Brainard, the exquisitely sophisticated wife of the distinguished specialist close by. Her graceful head, with its slight and becoming touches of gray at the temples, rested like a fine cameo against the warm hue of the cushion. Her brilliant eyes reflected the dancing firelight; her shapely hands, jewelled like Mrs. Breckenridge's, but after an even more rare and perfectly chosen fashion, lay in her silken lap.   As his glance fell upon these hands some whimsical thought brought to Brown's mind Mrs. Kelcey's red, work-roughened ones.　He wondered if by any chance the two hands would ever meet, and whether Mrs. Brainard's would shrink from the contact, or meet it as that of a sister, "under the skin."

Near her his sister Sue's dainty elegance of person showed like a flower against the big figure of Doctor Brainard, who sat at her elbow. Brainard himself, with his splendid head and erect carriage, was always an imposing personage; he had never seemed more so than now, with the face of Patrick Kelcey, Andrew Murdison, and James Benson, the little watchmaker, in the background of Brown's mind with which to contrast it.　Beyond Mrs. Brainard lounged Hugh Breckenridge—as nearly as one could be said to lounge—in a plain, cane-seated chair without arms.

At one side of the group was Webb Atchison, the rich bachelor of the party where all were possessed of wealth in plenty.　Next Atchison sat Miss Helena Forrest, the one member of the company who had not known where she was going until well upon her way there.   Upon her the glance of the man standing by the chimney-piece fell least often, yet there was no person present of whom he was so unremittingly conscious.   It may be said that from the moment that he had lifted her veil in his puzzled search for her identity, he had been conscious of little else.

There was not a single movement of Miss Forrest's hands—and she had certain little delightful, highly characteristic ways of helping out her speech with slight yet significant motions—but had its place in Brown's memory.   She was not a frequent talker, she did not speak one word to Sue Breckenridge's fifty; but when she did speak, in her voice of slow music, people listened. And yet one never thought of her, Brown remembered, as a silent person; the effect of her presence in any circle was that of a personality

of the active, not the passive, sort.   The eyes of
one speaking must, involuntarily, be drawn to
her because she was listening, if I may coin a
phrase, vividly.   As for her looks—she possessed that indescribable charm which is not
wholly a matter of beautiful features, but lies
rather in such details as the lift of the eyebrow,
the curve of the lip, the droop of the hair upon
the brow.   She was dressed much more simply
than either of the older women present, yet with
the simplicity, it must be admitted, of the artist.
She seemed somehow to make their goodly showing fade before her own, as a crimson flower
draws from the colour of one of delicate blue.

Well, take them separately or as a group,
they were an absorbing study to the man who
had seen so little of their kind for so long past,
yet knew that kind by the wontedness of his life-
time.   He seemed to himself somehow to be
viewing them all, for the first time, from a van-
tage point he had never before occupied.   Every

word they said in their pleasantly modulated, well-bred voices, with the familiar accent of the educated environment from which they came, and from which he came—it was his accent, too, but somehow it sounded a bit foreign to him to-night—struck upon his ear with a new meaning. Each gesture they made, personal and familiar to him as they were, struck Brown now with its special individuality.

"It's not fair, Don," said Sue Breckenridge suddenly, "for you to stand over there in the shadow and watch us, without our being able to see your face at all."

"You don't realize," declared Brown, in answer to this assertion and the general assenting laugh which followed it, backed by Atchison's "Hear, hear!" "that the group you all make in the light of my fire is a picture far ahead of anything in Atchison's collection. I should be an unappreciative host indeed if I didn't make the most of it."

"What an artful speech!" laughed Mrs. Brainard, lifting fine eyes in an attempt to make out the shadowy face above her. "It's well calculated to distract our attention from the fact that you are not changing your position by so much as the moving of an arm. We came to see you, man, not to show ourselves to you."

"We came to cheer his loneliness," put in Hugh Breckenridge with a peculiar, cynical-sounding little laugh for which he was famous. "And we find him up to his neck in boys. Jove! How do you stand their dirty hands, Don? That's what would get me, no matter how good my intentions were."

"Those hands were every pair scrubbed to a finish, to-day, in honour of Thanksgiving. Do you think we have no manners here?" retorted Brown.

"That wasn't the dinner party you wrote me of when you refused to come to mine, was it, Don?" questioned his sister.

"No.   This was an after-dinner party, partaking of the 'lavin's,'" Brown explained. "The real one was over an hour before."

"Do tell us about it.   Did you enjoy it? Won't you describe your guests?" Mrs. Brainard spoke eagerly.

"With pleasure.   The Kelceys are my next-door neighbours on the left.   Mrs. Kelcey is pure gold—in the rough.   Her husband is not quite her equal, but he knows it and strives to be worthy of her.   The Murdisons, on the other side, are—Scotch granite—splendid building material.   Old Mr. Benson, the watchmaker, is —well, he's full-jewelled.   The others I perhaps can't characterize quite so easily, but among them I find several uncut gems of the semi-precious varieties.   Of course there's considerable commonplace material—if you can ever call the stuff of which human beings are made com-- monplace, which I doubt.   There's more or less copper and brass, with a good bit of clay—as there is in all of us. And a deal of a more spiritual element which can't be measured or described, but which makes them all worth knowing."

He had spoken in a thoughtful tone, as if he took Mrs. Brainard's question seriously and meant to answer it in the same way. A moment's silence followed. Then Doctor Brainard said slowly:

"I suppose you don't find those priceless elements among the people of your abandoned parish. Down there we're all copper and clay, eh?"

"If you had been clay I might have done more with you," was the quick retort.

"And you can do things with these people, can you? Dig out the rough gold, polish the uncut diamonds, build temples of the granite—and perhaps mold even the clay into works of art?"

The answer to the ironic question was grave enough, and it came with a quietness which spoke more eloquently than fervid tones would have done of the feeling behind it.

"No, Doctor, I can't hope to do those things. I'm not wise enough. But the things these people are going to do to me, if I'll let them, are worth coming for."

"They've done some of them already," murmured Mrs. Brainard. But nobody heard her except Sue Breckenridge, who cried out:

"And you're not a bit homesick, Don, while you're living like this?"

"If you people won't come up here very often and make me remember what being with you is like, I shall get on pretty well," said Brown's voice from the shadow.

"Then we'll come as often as we can," cried Sue triumphantly.

"No, you won't—not if you want to help me. My reputation as an indigent bachelor out of a job won't stand many onslaughts of company dressed as you are. If you want to come to see me you must come disguised. I'm afraid I'm under suspicion already."

"Explain to them that we're the clay, they the uncut diamonds. That will let you out," advised Doctor Brainard grimly.

"Ah, but you don't look the part," said Brown, laughing. "You look like what you are, a big jewel of a fellow, as my friend Mrs. Kelcey would say. To tell the truth, you all seem like jewels to me to-night—and such polished ones you dazzle my eyes. Hugh, I'd forgotten what a well-cut coat looked like. I remember now."

"You seem pretty well dressed yourself," remarked Atchison, peering up into the shadow. "According to Mrs. Breckenridge, you go about dressed in monk's cloth, and a shabby variety at that. This doesn't look like it."

"He was wearing a dreadful, old shiny serge suit when I saw him a fortnight ago," said Sue. "And such a scarf-pin! Don, are you wearing that same scarf-pin to-night? Do show it to them."

"Does choosing to live by himself make a man a fair target for all the quips and arrows of his friends?" Brown queried, at the same time withdrawing obediently the little silver pin from his cravat and giving it into Atchison's outstretched hand. "Be just to that pin, Webb. It was given me by a special friend of mine."

"How will you exchange?" Atchison inquired gravely, touching his own neckwear as he examined the pin. A rare and costly example of the jeweller's art reposed there, as might have been expected.

"I'll not exchange, thank you."

"Neither will I," declared Atchison, leaning back with a laugh and passing the pin on down the line.

Hugh Breckenridge gave the obviously cheap and commonplace little article one careless glance, and handed it to Miss Forrest. She examined it soberly, as if seeking to find its peculiar value in its owner's eyes Then she looked at Brown.

"This has a story, I am sure, or you wouldn't care so much for it," she said. "Are we worthy to hear it, Mr. Brown?"

His eyes met hers, though as he stood she could barely make out that fact.

"I should like you to hear it."

"Come out of the darkness, Don, please!" begged his sister again.

The others echoed the wish, and Brown, yielding against his will—somehow he had never wanted more to remain in the shadow—took a chair at one end of the hearth, where he was in full view of them all.

"It was given me," said Brown, speaking in a tone which instantly arrested even Hugh Breckenridge's careless attention, though why it did so he could not have said, "by a man whose son was wearing it when he stood on a plank between two windows, ten stories up in the air, and passed fifteen girls over it to safety. Then —the plank burned through at one end. He had known it would."

There fell a hush upon the little group. Mrs. Brainard put out her hand and touched Brown's shoulder caressingly.

"No wonder you wouldn't exchange it, Don," she said, very gently.

"Was the father at your dinner, Don?" Doctor Brainard asked, after a minute.

"Yes, Doctor."

"So you wore it to please him," commented Sue.

"He wore it," said Helena Forrest, "as a man might wear the Victoria Cross."

"Ah, but I didn't earn it," denied Brown, without looking up.

"I'm not so sure of that," Mrs. Brainard declared. "You must have done something to make the father feel you worthy to wear a thing he valued so much."

"He fancied," said Brown—"he and the mother—that there was a slight resemblance between my looks and those of the son. And they have a finer memorial of him than anything he wore; they have one end of the burned plank. The father has cut the date on it, with his son's name, and it hangs over the chimney-piece."

"What a tragic thing!" cried Sue, shuddering. "I don't see how they can keep it. Do tell us something else, Don. Doesn't anything amusing ever happen here? Oh— what became of the baby?"

Brown rose suddenly to his feet. "I'm forgetting my hospitality," said he. "I'm going to make you all some coffee. The baby, Sue, is at Mrs. Kelcey's, next door. Having only six of her own, she could easily make room for the seventh."

"Tell us about the baby," demanded Webb

Atchison. "Has Don gone into the nursery business, with all the rest?"

Sue began to tell the story, describing the night on which she made her first visit to her brother. Brown disappeared into the kitchen and soon returned, bringing with him, as was his entertaining custom, the materials for brewing his coffee upon the hob.

"You remember," he said, as he came, "the way this room was cleared for your reception?"

"By an avalanche of boys, who swept everything, hurly-burly, into outer darkness," supplied Breckenridge.

"You can guess, perhaps, what the kitchen must be looking like, can't you?"

"Indescribable," murmured Sue. "You're not going to invite us to put it in order for you, are you, Don?—and wash all those dreadful, gaudy plates and cups?"

"Just take a look out there, will you?"

Sue shook her head, but Mrs. Brainard went

to the door, followed by Atchison and Miss Forrest. They looked out upon a low-ceiled, lamp-lighted room, in absolute order, in which was not a trace of the late festival-making except the piles of clean dishes upon the table, under which lay Bim, nose on paws, alert eyes on the strangers.

"Magic?" queried Mrs. Brainard. "Surely those noisy boys couldn't accomplish such a miracle?"

"Never. Though I suspect they were put to work by a good general, for the borrowed chairs are gone and so are several other bulky articles. There's no difficulty in guessing who did the deed," said Brown, busy with his coffee-making.

He served his guests presently with a beverage which made Atchison exclaim: "The old chap certainly knows how to make the best stuff I ever drank. When I tasted this brew first I invited myself to come out and stay a week with him, but he wouldn't have me."

"You're too polished an article for his hand; he wants his work-stuff raw," Doctor Brainard said again. Evidently this point rankled. Brown looked up.

"I'll challenge you to stay and have it out with me, Doctor," said he.

"Thank you, I came for no other purpose," retorted the doctor coolly. "These people brought me up to have a look at you, and I'm not going back till morning."

"That's great!" Brown's face showed his pleasure.

XI

BROWN'S PRESENT WORLD

When Miss Forrest returned from her survey of the kitchen she had come straight to the corner of the hearth where Brown stood, and had taken the chair beside the one he had lately occupied. He was therefore beside her when he sat down to drink his coffee with his guests. At a moment when Webb Atchison and Sue Breckenridge were engaged in a bit of controversy over the relative merits of varying methods of coffee making, Helena Forrest turned to Brown, who had been looking into the fire without speaking.

"I hope you don't really mind our coming up here to-night," she said.

"Mind it? If I did, I couldn't blame you, for you came against your will," he answered—and his eyes were no longer upon the fire.

"Without my consent, but not, perhaps, against my will."

He regarded her intently. She met his look without turning aside.

"You felt a curiosity to see the hermit in his cell," was his explanation of the matter.

She nodded. "Of course. Who wouldn't, after such reports as Mrs. Breckenridge brought back?"

"And now that you have seen him—you are consumed with pity?"

"No. If I am consumed with anything it is with envy."

His low laugh spoke his disbelief. She read it in the sound and in the way his gaze left her face and went back to the fire.

"You don't think I mean that," said she.

"Hardly."

"Why not?"

"It is—inconceivable."

"Why?"

Her face, turned toward him, invited him to look at it again, but he did not—just then.

"Because you are—Helena Forrest," he answered.

"And what is she, please, in your opinion?"

"An inhabitant of another world than that I live in."

"A world of which you have an even poorer opinion than you used to have when you lived in it yourself!"

He smiled. "Anyhow, I am no longer in it. Nor ever shall go back."

A startled look passed over her face. "You don't mean that you intend to stay here—forever?"

"Not quite that. But I mean to do this sort of work, rather than the sort I began with. To do it I must live much as I am living now, where-ever that may be.   Now—what about the envy of me you profess?"

He turned, still smiling, at the little sound he caught from her half-closed lips.

"Are you happy in such a decision?" she mur-mured.

"Do I look like an unhappy man?"

She shook her head.   "That's what I have been noticing about you ever since I came.   You did look unhappy when you went away.   Now, you don't.   And it is the look on your face which gives me the sense of envy."

Brown gave one quick glance at the rest of the party.   "Do you mean to say," he questioned, very low, "that you are not happy?"

"Does that seem so strange?"

"It might very naturally seem so, to one who knows what you have to make you the happiest of the happy."

"You yourself didn't find happiness among

similar surroundings," she said, looking at him intently.

"Similar?" The thought seemed to amuse him.

"Well, weren't they similar? At any rate we were in the same world, and you say now we are not."

"We are so far apart," said he evenly, "that we can only signal to each other. And even then—neither is familiar with the other's code!"

"Oh!" she exclaimed, and a strange expression showed in her eyes. "What a hard, hard thing for you to say! It doesn't sound like you."

"Hard?" he questioned, with a contraction of the brows. "It is substantially what you your-self once said. If it was true then, it must be true now."

Moved by some impulse the two looked at each other searchingly, Donald Brown's face grave but tense, Helena Forrest's full of a proud pain. Clearly they were not understanding each other's code now—so much was evident.

At this instant, without warning, the outer door flew open. Mrs. Kelcey, her round red face disordered, her breath coming short, stood upon the threshold and spoke pantingly, without regard to the company assembled:

"Mr. Brown, sor! The baby's dyin —the sthranger child. It was took all of a suddint. Would ye moind comin' to say a bit of a prayer over him? Father McCarty's away, or I wouldn't ask it."

She was gone with the words. With the first sentence Brown had sprung to his feet. As Mary Kelcey vanished he turned to Doctor Brainard.

"Come, Doctor," he said, with a beckoning hand. "While I say the bit of a prayer you try what you can do to keep the baby here!"

The eminent physician rose rather slowly to his feet. "It's probably no use," he demurred. "The woman knows."

"The Lord knows, too," declared Brown, with a propelling hand on his friend's arm: "knows that you're here to give the child a chance. Come! Hurry!"

The two went out. Doctor Brainard would have stayed for his hat and overcoat, but Brown would brook no delay.

Left behind, the party by the fire looked at one another with faces sobered. Hugh Brecken-ridge consulted his watch.

"It's time we were off," he declared. "The Doctor's going to stay anyway, and it's no use waiting for Don to come back."

"That's right," agreed Webb Atchison. "I came up here once before, about six months ago, and I saw then enough of the way things went here to know that he lives at the beck and call of every man, woman, and child in this district—and they call him, too. He'd just finished sobering up a drunkard that night, or scant attention I'd have had. Well, I'll walk

Mrs. Kelcey, her round face disordered, her breath coming short, stood upon the threshold

down to the hotel and send back Rogers and the car.   Be ready in ten minutes?"

They said they would be ready.   But in Brown's little bedroom, donning furry wraps, Helena Forrest spoke in Sue Breckenridge's ear:

"I can't bear to go till we know how it comes out."

Sue stared at her.   "You don't mean to say you care?   Why—it's just a forlorn little found-ling—better dead than alive.   I saw it when I was here two weeks ago.   It has nothing to live for, dear.   Don't think of it again."

"But he cared—your brother cared," said Helena Forrest.

"Oh, Don cares about everything.   I never saw such a soft heart.   Of course I think it's lovely of him, though I don't understand how he can be so absorbed in such a class of people."

Miss Forrest went to the one window of the room.   She lifted the plain shade which covered it and looked out into the night.

Ten yards away she saw a brightly lighted, un-curtained window, beyond which were figures, plainly discernible. The figures were moving, one bringing a pail, another stooping—the scene was not one of still waiting but of tense action. She caught a glimpse of Doctor Brain-ard's tall form bending above something at one side, then she saw Brown himself cross the room in haste.

Mrs. Brainard and Sue went back to the outer room to stand before the fire with the purpose of accumulating all the bodily heat possible before the long, cold drive. Miss Forrest, unheeding them, remained by the window in the unlighted bedroom. Minutes passed. Hugh Brecken-ridge had fallen to examining the larger room's eighteenth century features—he was something of a connoisseur in antiques.

Helena, turning from the window for a mo-ment, scanned the shadowy room in which she stood. It was very scantily furnished with the bare essentials.   Upon the plain chest of drawers which held Brown's bachelor belongings stood a few simply framed photographs; an old set of hanging bookshelves was crammed full of books, with more overflowing upon the floor.

Suddenly, as she stood there, an outer door banged; swift footsteps crossed the floor. Helena turned to see Donald Brown himself rushing into the room.   He ran to the chest of drawers, pulled one open, searched a minute, withdrew something, and was hurrying out of the room again, when he caught sight of the figure at the window.   Involuntarily he halted for an instant.

"Can you save it?" Helena cried, under her breath.

"I don't know—Brainard's got his coat off. Pray for us, will you?"

He was gone again.

Beside the narrow bed on which he lay every night, there dropped upon its knees a figure in

sumptuous furs; a face such as men vow themselves ready to die for was pressed into the hard
little pillow. Helena Forrest breathed a prayer of
beseeching for a life she had never seen, and when
she had done lifted eyes wet with tears.

As Hugh Breckenridge, protesting at the late-
ness of the hour, marshalled his friends into the
great car at the door, Doctor Brainard came out
of Mrs. Kelcey's house and ran across to the curb.

"Don wants me to tell you that the baby's
pulled through. It's gone off to sleep with his
finger in its fist, and he won't leave it. He says
'good-night' to you."

"Was it the prayer or the potion that saved it,
Doctor?" questioned Breckenridge in his caustic
tone.

"I don't know," said the doctor—and there
was something new and gentle in his voice. "It
was very nearly beyond potions—I'm inclined to
think it was the prayer."

An hour afterward, Doctor Brainard, sitting

wide-awake and thoughtful before Brown's fire, was aware of the quiet entrance of the younger man. He looked up, and a radiant smile met him.

"Still doing well, I see, Don."

Brown nodded. He sank down into the chair opposite the doctor and ran his hand through his hair. In spite of the brightness of his face the gesture betrayed weariness.

Doctor Brainard got up. He went over to the corner where his overcoat hung upon a peg in the wall, and took from a pocket a small instrument composed mostly of tubes. He inserted certain earpieces in his ears and returned to the fire.

"Sit up and let me get at you," he commanded.

Brown glanced round, saw the doctor's grotesque appearance with the stethoscope in position, and shook his head.

"That's not fair. I was up rather early, and

it's been a fairly full day—and night.   Take me in the morning."

"I'll take you right now, when you're tired enough to show up whatever's there.   Coat off, please."

He made his examination painstakingly, omitting no detail of his inquiry into the state of both heart and lungs.

"What would you say if I told you you were in a bad way?" he asked.

Brown smiled.   "I shouldn't believe you.   I know you too well.   You can't disguise the fact that you find nothing new, and the old things improved.   I know I'm stronger than I was a year ago.   Why shouldn't I be—with nothing to do but take care of myself?"

The doctor whistled.   "How do you make that out, that 'nothing to do?'"

"With the demands of a great parish off my shoulders the little I do here is child's play."

"After I left you with the baby," said the

doctor, "Mrs. Kelcey followed me into the other room and told me a few things.   In your old parish you had your sleep o' nights.   In your new one I should say you spend the sleeping hours in activity."

"In my old parish," said Brown, studying the fire with an odd twist at the corners of his lips, "I lay awake nights worrying over my problems. Here, I'm asleep the minute my head touches the pillow.   Isn't that a gain?"

"Too weary to do anything else, I suppose. Well, I shall have to admit that you are improved—surprisingly so.   You are practically well.   But what I can't understand is how a man of your calibre, your tastes, your fineness of make-up, can stand consorting with these people. Be honest, now.   After such a visit as you've had to-night with the old friends, don't you feel a bit like giving in and coming back to us?"

Brown lifted his head.   "Doctor," said he, slowly, and with a peculiar emphasis which made his friend study his face closely, "if the Devil wanted to put temptation in my way, just as I have decided on my future course, he did it by sending you and the others down here to-night. If I could have jumped into that car with the rest of you, and by that one act put myself back in the old place, I would have done it—but for one thing. And that's the sure knowledge that soft living makes me soft. I love the good things of this life so that they unfit me for real service. Do you know. what was the matter with my heart when I came away? I do. ∶ It was high living. It was sitting with my legs under the mahogany of my millionaire parish-ioners' tables, driving in their limousines, drinking afternoon tea with their wives, letting them send me to Europe whenever I looked a bit pale. Soft! I was a down pillow, a lump of putty. I, who was supposed to be a fighter for the Lord!"

"Nonsense, man!" cried the doctor, now thoroughly aroused. "You were the hardest worker in the city. Your organizations—your charities——"

"My organizations, my charities!" The words came in a tone of contempt. "They were all in fine working order when I came to them. They continued to work, with no help from me. They are working quite as well now in my absence as they did in my presence. St. Timothy's is a great, strong society of the rich, and the man they engage to preach to them on Sundays has mighty little to do that any figurehead couldn't do as well. Down here—well, there is something to do which won't get done unless I do it. And if this neighbourhood, or any other similar one, needs me, there's no question that still more do I need the neighbourhood."

"In other words," said the doctor, "Mrs. Kelcey can do more for you than Bruce Brainard?"

The look which met his frown was comprehending. "Doctor," said Brown, "every man

knows his own weakness.   I like the society of
Bruce Brainard so well that when I'm in it I can
forget all the pain and sorrow in the world.
When I'm with Mrs. Kelcey I have to remember
the hurt, and the grind, and the hardness of life
—and it's good for me.   It helps me, as St. Paul
said, to '*keep under my body and bring it into sub-
jection.*'"

"That's monkish doctrine."

"No, it's St. Paul's, I tell you.   Remember
the rest of it?—'*lest that by any means, when I
have preached to others, I myself should be a castaway!*'"

"You!   A castaway!"   The doctor laughed.

Brown nodded, rising.   "You can see a long
way into a man's body, Doctor, but not so far
into his soul.   There's been a pretty rotten
place in mine.   .   .   .   Come, shall we go to
bed?   It's almost two."

The doctor assented, and Brown went into his
bedroom to make it ready for his guest.   Closing

the drawers he had opened in such haste two hours before, his eye was caught by something unfamiliar. Against one of the framed photographs which stood upon the top of the chest leaned a new picture, unframed. By the light of the small lamp he had brought into the room he examined it. As the face before him was presented to his gaze he stopped breathing for the space of several thudding heartbeats.

Out of the veiling brown mists of the picture looked a pair of eyes at which one glance had long been of more moment to him than the chance to look long and steadily into other eyes. The exquisite lines of a face which, having seen, men did not forget, were there before him, in his possession. It was the face of the woman, young and rich with beauty and with worldly wealth, who had, three years before, refused to marry Donald Brown.

"How did this come here? Did Sue leave it? Or did *you*?" He questioned the photograph in his mind, staring at it with eager eyes. "Wasn't it enough for you to come here to-night, to make me realize how far apart we are? You like to play with men's hearts—so they say. Don't you think it's a bit cruel to play with mine —now?"

But he looked and looked at the enchanting face. And even as he looked Doctor Brainard called out from the other room:

"By the way, Don, I suppose you've noticed that Atchison seems to be getting on with his suit. Everybody thinks it's either an engagement or likely to be one soon. Pretty fine match, eh?"

It was a full minute before the answer came. When it did it sounded a little as if the speaker had his head in the clothespress which opened from the small bedroom, albeit the tone was gay enough:

"Webb's one of the best men I know. He deserves to win whatever he wants. Do you like a hard pillow or a soft, Doctor?"

XII

BROWN'S OLD WORLD

On a certain morning in February, Mrs. Hugh Breckenridge alighted in haste from her limousine in front of a stately apartment house in the best quarter of a great city. She hurried through the entrance hall to the lift and was taken up with smooth speed to the seventh story. In a minute more she was eagerly pressing the button at the door of a familiar suite of rooms into which she had not had occasion to enter for more than a year, for the very good reason that they had been closed and unoccupied in the absence of their tenant.

The returned tenant himself opened the door to her, a tall figure looming in the dusk of an unlighted corridor—a tall figure infinitely dear to Sue Breckenridge.

"O Don!" cried the visitor in an accusing tone. "How could you come back without letting us know?"

"I've been back only an hour," explained Donald Brown, submitting to and warmly returning his sister's embrace. "How in the world did you hear of it so soon? Did Brainard——"

She nodded. "Mrs. Brainard called me up at once, of course. She knew you couldn't be serious in trying to keep people from knowing you were here, least of all your sister!"

"I was intending to come to you before luncheon; I only meant to surprise you. As for the rest—I should be glad if they needn't know; at least until I'm ready to leave."

"To leave! Don! You're not going to persist in going back! It can't be true! You won't give up this apartment—tell me you won't!"

His sister's tone was anguished. Before he answered Brown led her into the library of the suite, the room in which he had been occupied when her ring came, and put her into a big arm-chair, taking from her her wrap and furs. Then he sat down upon the edge of a massive mahogany writing-table near by, crossing his long legs and folding his arms, while she mutely waited for him to speak.

"Sue," he said—and his face had in it a sort of reflection of the pain in hers—"you may be sure I haven't come to this decision without a deal of thought. But I've made it, and I'm going to stick to it because I believe it's the thing for me to do. I assure you that since I came into these rooms they have been beseeching me, as loudly as inanimate things can, not to desert them. I'm going to find it the hardest task of my life to take leave of them."

"Don't take leave of them! Lock them up for another year, if you must persist in your experiment, but don't, *don't* burn your bridges behind you! Oh, how can you think of leaving your splendid church and going off to consign yourself to oblivion, living with poor people the rest of your days? You—*you*—Don!—I can't believe it of you!"

His face, in his effort at repression, grew stern. His folded arms became tense in the muscles.

"Don't make it harder for me than it is. I can't discuss it with you, because though I argued till I was dumb I could never make you see what I see. Accept my decision, Sue dear, and don't try my soul by pleading with me. . . . I have a lot to do. I should like your help. See here, would you care to have any of my things? Look about you. This is rather a good rug under your feet. Will you have it—and any others you fancy?"

She looked down at the heavy Eastern rug, exquisite in its softness and richness of colouring.

It was one of which, knowing its value, she had long envied her brother the possession. She put up her hand and brushed away the mist from her eyes.

"Aren't you going to take *any* comfortable things with you? Are you going to go on living on pine chairs and rag carpets—you, who were brought up on rugs like this?"

He nodded. "For the most part. I've been wondering if I might indulge myself in one big easy chair, just for old times. But I'm afraid it won't do."

"Oh, mercy, Don! Why *not?*"

"How should I explain its presence, opposite my red-cushioned rocker? Give it a good look, Sue, that chair, and tell me honestly if I can afford to introduce such an incongruous note into my plain bachelor house up there."

She surveyed the chair in question, a luxurious and costly type standing for the last word in masculine comfort and taste. It was one which had been given to Brown by Webb Atchison, and had long been a favourite.

"Oh, I don't know," she said hopelessly, shaking her head. "I can't decide for any monk what he shall take into his cell."

Brown flushed, a peculiar dull red creeping up under his dark skin. He smothered the retort on his lips, however, and when he did speak it was with entire control, though there was, nevertheless, an uncompromising quality in his inflection which for the moment silenced his sister as if he had laid his hand upon her mouth.

"Understand me, once for all, Sue—if you can. I am going into no monastery. To such a man as I naturally am, I am going out of what has been a sheltered life into one in the open. You think of me as retiring from the world. Instead of that, I am just getting into the fight. And to fight well—I must go stripped."

She shook her head again and walked over to

the window, struggling with very real emotion. At once he was beside her, and his arm was about her shoulders. He spoke very gently now.

"Don't take it so hard, dear girl. I'm not going to be so far away that I can never come back. You will see me from time to time. I couldn't get on without my one sister—with father and mother gone, and the brothers at the other side of the world. Come, cheer up, and help me decide what disposal to make of my stuff. Will you take the most of it?"

She turned about, presently, dried her eyes determinedly, and surveyed the room. It was a beautiful room, the sombre hues of its book-lined walls relieved by the rich and mellow tones of its rugs and draperies, the distinguished furnishings of the writing-table, and the subdued gleam of a wonderful reading-lamp of wrought copper which had been given to Brown by Sue herself.

"If you will let me," she said, "I'll give up one room to your things and put all these into it. Aren't you even going to take your books?"

"I must—a couple of hundred, at least. I can't give up such old friends as these."

"A couple of hundred—out of a couple of thousand!"

"There are five thousand in this room," said Brown cheerfully. "But two hundred will give me a very good selection of favourites, and I can change them from time to time. I have sixty or seventy already with me. . . . Hello! Who can that be? Has Brainard been giving me away right and left?"

He answered the ring, and admitted Webb Atchison, rosy of cheek and rather lordly of appearance, as always. The bachelor came in, frowning even as he smiled, and bringing to Donald Brown a vivid suggestion of old days.

"Caught!" he cried, shaking hands.

"Thought you could sneak in and out of town like a thief in the night, did you? It can't be done, old man."

He was in a hurry and could stay but ten minutes. Five of those he devoted to telling Brown what he thought of the news he had heard, by which he understood that St. Timothy's was to lose permanently the man whom it had expected soon to have back. Brown listened with head a little down-bent, arms folded again, lips set in lines of determination. He had been fully prepared for the onslaughts of his friends, but that fact hardly seemed to make it easier to meet them. When Atchison had delivered himself uninterrupted, Brown lifted his head with a smile.

"Through, Webb?" he asked.

"No, I'm not through, by a long shot, but it's all I have time for now, for I came on a different matter. Since I heard you were here I've been telephoning around, and I've got together a little dinner-party for to-night that you won't evade if you have a particle of real affection for me. I'm not going to be cheated out of it. It'll be a hastily arranged affair, but there may be something decent to eat and drink. Brainard tells me you're not going to linger in town an hour after your business is done, so I thought best to lose no time. You'll come, of course? The way you're looking just now I don't know but you're equal to refusing me even such a small favour as this one!"

Brown crossed the room, to lay his hands on Atchison's shoulders. His eyes were dark with suppressed feeling.

"My dear old friend," said he affectionately, "I wish you wouldn't take the thing this way. I'm not dealing blows at those I love; if I'm dealing them at anybody it's at myself. I can't possibly tell you what it means to me—this crisis. I can only ask you not to think hardly of me. As for the dinner, if it will please you to have me agree to it I will, only—I should a little rather have you stand me up against a wall and take a shot at me!"

"For a deserter?"

Atchison spoke out of his grief and anger, not from belief in the motive he imputed. When he saw Donald Brown turn white and clench the hands he dropped from his friend's shoulders, Atchison realized what he had done. He winced under the sting of the quick and imperious command which answered him:

"Take that back, Webb!"

"I do—and apologize," said the other man instantly, and tears smarted under his eyelids. "You know I didn't mean it, Don. But—hang it all!—I'm bitterly disappointed and I can't help showing it."

"Disappointed in me—or in my act?" Brown was still stern.

"In your act, of course. I'm bound to acknowledge that it must take a brave man to cut cables the way you're doing—a mighty brave man."

"I don't care about being considered brave, but I won't be called a coward."

"I thought," said Atchison, trying to smile, "there was something in your Bible about turning the other cheek."

"There is," said Brown steadily. "And I do it when I come to your dinner. But between now and then I'll knock you down if you insult the course I've laid out for myself."

The two men gazed at each other, the one the thorough man of the world with every sign of its prospering touch upon him, the other looking somehow more like a lean and hardened young soldier of the army than a student of theology. Both pairs of eyes softened. But it was Atchison's which gave way first.

"Confound you, Don—it's because of that splendidly human streak in you that we love you here. You've always seemed to have enough personal acquaintance with the Devil and his works to make you understand the rest of us, and refrain from being too hard on us."

At which Sue Breckenridge—who had been listening with tense-strung nerves to the interview taking place in her presence—laughed, with an hysterical little sob shaking her. Both men looked at her.

"Poor Sue," said Brown. "She doesn't like to have you quarrel with me, yet it's all she can do to keep from quarrelling with me herself! Between you, if you don't undermine my purpose, it will be only because I've been preparing my defenses for a good while and have strong patrols out at the weak points."

"I give you fair warning. I'll undermine it yet if I can," and Atchison gripped Brown's hand with fervor before he went away, charging Sue Breckenridge with the responsibility of bringing her brother to the dinner to be given that evening.

"Now, what"—said Brown, turning to his

writing-table when Atchison had gone, and ab-
sently picking up a bronze paper-weight which
lay there—"put it into his head to fire a dinner
at me the moment he knew I was here?"

"We all have a suspicion," said Sue, watching
him as she spoke, "that he and Helena are ready
to announce their engagement. It may have
popped into his head that with you here it was
just the time to do it. Of course," she went on
hurriedly, in answer to something she thought
she saw leap into her brother's face, "we don't
absolutely know that they're engaged. He's
been devoted for a good while, and since he's
never been much that sort with women it looks
as if it meant something."

"It looks it on his part," said Brown, opening
a drawer in the table and appearing to search
therein. "Does it look it on hers?"

"Not markedly so. But Helena's getting on
—she must be twenty-six or seven—and she always seems happy with him. Of course that's

no evidence, for she has such a charmingly clever way with men you never can tell when she's bored—and certainly they can't. It's just that it seems such a splendidly fitting match we're confident there's ground for our expectations."

"I see. Altogether, that dinner promises well for sensations—of one sort or another. Meanwhile, shall we pitch into business?"

Together they went through Brown's apartment, which was a large one, and comprised everything which he had once considered necessary to the comfort of a bachelor establishment. As he looked over that portion of the place pertaining to the cooking and serving of food he smiled rather grimly at the contrast it inevitably brought to his mind. Standing before the well-filled shelves in the butler's pantry he eyed a certain cherished set of Sèvres china, thinking of the cheap blue-and-white ware which now filled all his needs, and recalling with a sense of amusement the days, not so long past, when he would have considered himself ill served had his breakfast appeared in such dishes.

"It's all in the way you look at it, Sue," he exclaimed, opening the doors of leaded glass and taking down a particularly choice example of the ceramic art in the shape of a large Satsuma plate. "Look at that, now! Why should a chop taste any better off that plate than off the one I ate from this morning at daybreak? It tastes no better—I vow it doesn't taste as good. I've a keener appetite now than last year, when Sing Lee, my Chinese cook, was cudgelling his Asiatic brains to tempt me."

"That's not the way I look at it," Sue answered mournfully. "To me it makes all the difference in the world how food is served, not to mention how it is cooked. Do you ever have anything but bacon and eggs at that dreadful place of yours?"

"Bless your heart, yes! I don't deny myself

good food, child—get that out of your mind. Why, just night before last Jennings and I had an oyster roast, on the half-shell, over the coals in my fireplace. My word, but they were good! If Webb can give us anything better than that to-night he'll surprise me."

"Who is Jennings? A laundryman or a policeman?"

"Neither. Jennings is a clerk in the office of a great wholesale hardware house. He was down on his luck, a while back, but he's pulled out of his trouble. When his wife's called out of town, as she often is by the old people back home, he keeps me company. He's particularly fond of roasted oysters, is Jennings, since a certain night when I introduced them to his unaccustomed palate. It's great fun to see him devour them."

Sue shook her head again. She could seem to do little else these days, being in a perpetual state of wonder and regret over that which she could not understand—quite as her brother had said. He sent her away an hour before luncheon time, telling her that he would follow when he had attended to certain matters in which she could not help. Having put her into her car, he waved a cheery hand at her as she drove away, and returned to his apartment. He lingered a little at the lift to ask after the welfare of the young man who operated it, whom he had known in past days; but presently he was in his library again with the door locked behind him. And here for a brief space business was suspended.

Before the big leather chair he fell upon his knees, burying his head in his arms.

"*Oh, good Father,*" said Brown, just above his breath, "*only Thou canst help me through this thing. It's even harder than I thought it would be. I want the old life, I want the old love—my heart is weak within me at the thought of giving them up. . . . I know the temptation comes not from without but from within. It's my own weak self, that is my enemy, not the lure of the life I'm giving up. . . . Give me strength— fighting strength. . . . Help me—'not to give in while I can stand and see.'"*

Presently he rose to his feet. He was pale, but in his face showed the renewed strength of purpose he had asked for. He set about the task of packing the few things he meant to take with him, working with a certain unhurried efficiency which accomplished no small amount in that hour before luncheon. Then he descended to find his sister's car waiting for him, and was whirled away.

XIII

BROWN'S TRIAL BY FLOOD

At nine o'clock that night, feeling a little as if he were in some sort of familiar dream, Brown, wearing evening dress for the first time in more than a year, sat looking about him. He was at Mrs. Brainard's right hand, in the post of the guest of honour, for Mrs. Brainard was playing hostess for her bachelor friend, Webb Atchison, in the apartment of the princely up-town hotel which was his more or less permanent home.

About the great round table were gathered a goodly company—the company of Brown's old friends among the rich and eminent of the city. Not only men of great wealth, but men distinguished in their professions, noted for their achievements, and honoured for their public services, were among those hurriedly asked to do this man honour. They had all been more or less constant members of his congregation during the years when he was making a name as the most forceful and fearless young preacher who ever ventured to tell the people of aristocratic St. Timothy's what he thought of them.

And they were gathered to-night to tell him what they thought of him. They were sparing no pains to do so. More than once, while he parried their attacks upon his resolution to leave them permanently, parried them with a smiling face, with a resolute quiet voice, with the quickness of return thrust for which he was famous in debate, he was inwardly sending up one oft-repeated, pregnant petition: *"Lord, help me through this—for Thy sake !"*

They were not men alone who combined

against him with every pressure of argument; there were women present who used upon him every art of persuasion. Not that of speech alone, but that subtler witchery of look and smile with which such women well know how to make their soft blows tell more surely than harder ones from other hands. Among these, all of whom were women of charm and distinction after one fashion or another, was one who alone, though she seemed to be making no direct attack, was waging the heaviest war of all against Donald Brown's determination.

Atchison, in arranging the places of his guests, had put Helena Forrest at Brown's right, at the sacrifice of his own pleasure, for by this concession she was farthest from himself. Whether or not he understood how peculiarly deadly was the weapon he thus used against his friend, he knew that Helena was capable of exerting a powerful influence upon any man—how should he himself not know it, who was at her feet? He

had no compunction in bringing that influence
to bear upon Brown at this moment, when the
actual word of withdrawal had not yet been
spoken.

Yet as from time to time Atchison looked toward these two of his guests he wondered if Helena
were doing all she could in the cause in which he
had enlisted her. She was saying little to
Brown, he could see that; and Brown was saying
even less to her. Each seemed more occupied
with the neighbour upon the farther side than
with the other. Just what this meant Atchison
could not be sure.

The dinner, an affair of surprising magnifi-
cence considering the brief hours of its preparation, drew at length to its close. It seemed to
Brown that he had been sitting at that table, in
the midst of the old environment in which he
had once been carelessly happy and assured, for
hours upon end, before the signal came at last
for the departure of the women. And even then

he knew that after they had gone the worst was probably to come.

It came. Left alone with him, the men of the party redoubled their attacks. With every argument, renewed and recast, they assaulted him. He withstood them, refusing at the last to argue, merely lifting his head with a characteristic gesture of determination, smiling wearily, and saying with unshaken purpose: "It's no use, gentlemen. I've made up my mind. I'm sorry you think I'm wrong, but I can't help that, since I believe I'm right."

They could not credit their own failure, these men of power, so accustomed to having things go their way that they were unable to understand even the possibility of being defeated. And they were being defeated by a man whom they had never admired more—and they had made him, as Sue Breckenridge had said, the idol of the great church—than now when he refused them. But they, quite naturally, did not show him that. They showed him disappointment, chagrin, cynicism, disbelief in his judgment, everything that could make his heart beat hard and painfully with the weight of their displeasure.

Suddenly he rose to his feet. A hush fell, for they thought he was going to speak to them. He was silent for a minute, looking down at these old friends who were so fond of him; then he opened his mouth. But not to speak—to sing.

It was a powerful asset of Donald Brown's, and it had never been more powerful than now, this voice which had been given him of heaven. They had often heard him before but now, under these strange circumstances, they listened with fresh amazement to the beauty of his tones. Every word fell clean-cut upon their ears, every note was rich with feeling, as Brown in this strange fashion made his plea, took his

stand with George Matheson's deathless words
of passionate loyalty:

> "Make me a captive, Lord,
> And then I shall be free;
> Force me to render up my sword,
> And I shall conqueror be.
> I sink in life's alarms
> When by myself I stand;
> Imprison me within Thy arms,
> And strong shall be my hand."

When they looked up, these men, they
saw that the women of the party had come
back to the doors, drawn by an irresistible
force.

In a strange silence, broken only by low-
spoken words, the whole company returned to
the living-rooms of the apartment. Here
Brown himself broke the spell he had laid upon
them.

Speaking in the ringing voice they knew of
old, and with a gesture of both arms outflung as

if he threw himself upon their friendship, he cried blithely:

"Ah, give me a good time now, dear people! Let me play I'm yours and you are mine again— just for to-night."

That settled it. Webb Atchison brought his hand down upon his victim's shoulder with a resounding friendly blow, calling:

"He's right. We've given him a bad two hours of it. Let's make it up to him, and let him have the right sort of send-off—since he will go. He will—there's no possible question of that. So let's part friends."

"I don't know," said Brown, smiling in the midst of the faces which now gave him back his smile, "but that if you are kind to me you'll test my endurance still more heavily. But—we'll risk it."

The scene now became a gay one—gay, at least, upon the surface. Brown was his old self again, the one they had known, and he was the centre of the good-fellowship which now reigned. So, for a time. Then came the supreme test of his life—as unexpectedly as such tests come, when a man thinks he has won through to the thin edge of the struggle.

XIV

BROWN'S TRIAL BY FIRE

He had gone alone into a den of Atchison's, where was kept a medley of books and pipes and weapons, a bachelor collection of trophies of all sorts. He was in search of a certain loving-cup which had been mentioned and asked for, and Atchison himself had for the moment left the apartment to see an insistent caller below. The den was at some distance from the place where the company was assembled, and Brown could hear their voices only in the remote distance as he searched.

Suddenly a light sound as of the movement of silken draperies fell upon his ear, and at the same instant a low voice spoke. He swung about, to see a figure before him at sight of which, alone as he had been with it for months, he felt his unsubdued heart leap in his breast. By her face he knew she had followed him for a purpose. He let her speak.

"Donald Brown," she said—and she spoke fast and breathlessly, as if she feared, as he did, instant interruption and this were her only chance—"what you have said to-night makes me forget everything but what I want you to know."

Quite evidently her heart was beating synchronously with his, for he could see how it shook her. He stared at her, at the lovely line and colour of cheek and chin, at the wonderful shadowed eyes, at the soft darkness of her heavy hair. She was wearing misty white to-night, with one great red rose upon her breast; she was such a sight as might well blind a man, even if he were not already blind with love of her. The fragrance of the rose was in his nostrils—it assailed his senses as if it were a part of her, its fragrance hers. But he did not speak.

"You asked me something once," she went on, with an evident effort. "Would you mind telling me if—if——"

But he would not help her. He could not believe he understood what she meant to say.

"You make it very hard for me," she murmured. "Yet I believe I understand why, if this thing is ever said at all, I must be the one to say it. Do you—Donald—do you—still—care?"

"*O God!*" he cried in his heart. "*O God! Couldn't You have spared me this?*"

But aloud, after an instant, he said, a little thickly, "I think you know without asking. I shall never stop caring."

She lifted her eyes. "Then——" and she waited.

He must speak. She had done her part. His head swam with the sudden astounding revelation that she was his for the taking, if—— Ah, but the *if!* He knew too well what that must mean.

"Are you tempting me, too?" he asked, with sudden fierceness. "Do you mean—like all the rest—I may havė you if—I give up my purpose and stay here?"

Mutely her eyes searched his. Dumb with the agony of it his searched hers in return. He turned away.

"Don!" Her voice was all low music. The words vibrated appealingly; she had seen what it meant to him. She put out one hand as if to touch him—and drew it back. "Listen to me, please. I know—I know—what a wonderful sacrifice you are making. I admire and honour you for it—I do. But—think once more. This great parish—surely there is work for you here, wonderful work. Won't you do it—*with me?*"

He looked at her with sudden decision on his course.

"You left that photograph?" He spoke huskily.

She nodded.

"You left it there, in my poor house. I've cherished it there. It hasn't suffered. You wouldn't suffer. Will you live—and work—with me—*there ?*"

"Oh!" She drew back. "How can you—— Do you realize what you ask?"

"I don't ask it expecting to receive it. I know it's impossible—from your viewpoint. But—it's—all I have to ask——"

He broke off, fighting savagely with the desire to seize her in his arms that was all but over-mastering him.

She moved away a step in her turn, standing with down-bent head, the partial line of her profile, the curve of her neck and beautiful shoulder, presenting an even greater appeal to the devouring flame of his longing than her eyes had done. It seemed to him that he would give the heart out of his body even to press his lips upon that fair flesh just below the low-drooping masses of her hair, flesh exquisite as a child's in contrast with the dark locks above it. All the long months of his exile pressed upon him with mighty force to urge him to assuage his loneliness with this divine balm.

Suddenly she spoke, just above a whisper. "I wonder," she said, "if any woman ever humiliated herself—like this—to be so refused."

He answered that with swift, eager words: "It is the most womanly, the most wonderful thing, any woman could do for a man. I shall never forget it, or cease to honour you for it. I love you—*love you*—for it—ten thousand times more than I loved you before, if that can be. I *must* say it. I must put it into words that you and I can both remember, or I think my heart will burst. But—Helena—I have vowed this vow to my God. I have put my hand to this plow. I can't turn back—not even for you. No man, having done that, '*and looking back, is fit for the kingdom of God.*' He isn't fit for the kingdoms of earth, either. He isn't fit for—hell!''

Very slowly she moved away from him, her head still drooping. At the door she did not pause and look back, actress-like, to try him with one more look. She went like a wounded thing. And at the sight, the wild impulse to rush after her and cry to her that nothing in the wide universe mattered, so that she should lift that head and lay it on his breast, gripped him and wrung him, till drops of moisture started out upon his forehead, and he turned sick. Then she was out of sight, and he stood grasping the back of a chair, fighting for control. This was a dinner-party—a dinner-party! Kind God in heaven! And he and she must go back to those other people and smile and talk, must somehow cover it all up. How was it conceivably to be done?

She could do it, perhaps. After all, it could

not be the soul-stirring thing to her that it was to him. She loved him enough to be his wife— under the old conditions. She did not love him enough to go with him as his wife into the new conditions. Then she could not be suffering as he was suffering. Wounded pride— she was feeling that, no doubt of it—wounded pride is not a pleasant thing to feel. She loved him somewhat, loved him enough to take the initiative in this scene to-night. But real love— she could not know what that was, or she would follow him to the ends of the earth. It was the woman's part to follow, not the man's. Hers to give up her preference for his duty. Since she could not do this, she did not really love him. This was the bitterest drop in the whole bitter cup!

Footsteps came rapidly along the corridor. Webb Atchison appeared in the doorway. At the first sound of his return Brown had wheeled and was found standing before a cabinet, in

"Are you tempting me, too?" he asked, with sudden fierceness

which behind glass doors was kept a choice collection of curios from all parts of the world.   He
was trying to summon words to explain that he
was looking for a certain loving-cup—*a loving-
cup*—when one had just been presented, full to
overflowing, to his thirsty lips, and he had refused to drink!

But Atchison was full of his message.

"Don, I've done my best to put the fellow off,
but he will see you.   Hang it!—to-night of all
nights!   I don't know why that following of
yours should pursue you to this place.   I suspect it will be considerable of a jolt to that chap
to see you in an expanse of white shirt-front.
But it seems somebody has been taken worse
since you left, and insists on seeing you.   Why
in thunder did you leave an address for them to
find you at?"

By the time Atchison had delivered himself of
all this Brown had hold of himself, could turn
and speak naturally.   The news had been like a

dash of cold water in the face of a fainting man.

"Who is worse—Mr. Benson?"

"Think that was the name—an old man. The messenger's waiting, though I told him you certainly couldn't go back to-night."

"I certainly shall go back to-night. Where is he?"

Expostulating uselessly, Atchison led the way. Brown found Andrew Murdison standing with a look of dogged determination on his face, which changed to one of relief when he saw Brown. Old Benson, the watchmaker, who had been convalescing from illness when Brown came away, had suffered a relapse and had probably but few hours to live.

With a brief leave-taking, in the course of which Brown held for an instant the hand of Helena Forrest and found it cold as ice in his grasp, he went away. As the train bore him swiftly back to the place he had left so recently, certain words came to him and stayed by him, fitting themselves curiously to the rhythmic roar of the train:

"God is faithful, who will not suffer you to be tempted above that ye are able; but will with the temptation also make a way to escape, that ye may be able to bear it."

And the car wheels, as they turned, seemed to be saying, mile after mile: *"A way to escape—a way to escape—a way to escape!"*

XV

BROWN'S BROWN STUDY

Standing in his kitchen doorway, Brown looked out into his back yard.

It was, in one way, an unusual back yard for that quarter of the city, and in that one way it differed from the back yards of his neighbours. While theirs were bounded on all sides by high and ugly board fences, his was encompassed by a stone wall standing even higher, and enclosing the small area of possibly forty feet by thirty in a privacy quite unknown elsewhere in the district. This stone wall had been laid by the Englishman who had built the house, his idea of having things to himself being the product of his early life in a country where not only is every man's house his castle, but the surrounding ground thereof, as well, his domain, from which he would keep out every curious eye.

It was an evening in mid-April. Brown had opened the big oak door to let the late western light of the spring day flood his kitchen, while he washed and put away the dishes lately used for his supper—and for that of a forlorn and ill-used specimen of tramp humanity who had arrived as he was sitting down.

He was presently to address a gathering of factory girls in a near-by schoolhouse; and he was trying, as he stood in the door, with the soft spring air touching gratefully his face, to gather his thoughts together for the coming talk. But he was weary with a long day's labours, and somehow his eyes could summon no vision of the faces he was to see. Instead——

"There ought to be a garden back here," he said to himself. "If I'm to stay here for the coming year—as it looks as if I must—I should cultivate this little patch and make it smile a bit. As it is, it's doing no good to anybody, not even Bim. He's pretty careless about his bones out here, and leaves them around instead of burying 'em decently. I must teach him better. This would be a good place to bring the children into, if it had some flowers in it."

The notion cheered him a little, as the thought of flowers in the spring has a way of doing. He made a rough plan of the garden, in his mind, laying out beds of sturdy bloom, training vines to cover the bleak expanse of stone, even planting a small tree or two of rapid growth—for the benefit of whomever should follow him as a tenant of the old house. Presently he closed the door with some sense of refreshment, mental and physical, and forced his thoughts into the channel it was now imperative they should occupy.

He took his way to the meeting in the school-house, however, with a step less rapid than was usually his. It might have been the enervating influence of the mild spring air; it might have been the pressure of certain recollections which he had not yet succeeded, in the two months which had passed since the farewell dinner at Webb Atchison's, in so putting aside that they should not often depress and at times even dominate his spirit. Though he had left the old life completely behind him, and had settled into the new with all the conviction and purpose he could summon, he was subject, especially when physically weary, as to-night, to a heaviness of heart which would not be mastered.

"But I must—*I must*—stiffen my back," he said sternly to himself, as he neared the dingy schoolhouse toward which, from all directions, he could see his audience making its way. It was not the first time he had addressed these girls and women, in so informal and unostentatious a manner that no one of his hearers had so much as suspected his profession, but had taken him for one of their own class. "He's got a way with him," they put it, "that makes you feel like you could listen to him all night." The sight of them now provided the stimulus he needed, and as he smiled and nodded at two or three whom he had personally met he felt the old interest in his task coming to his aid.

And in a brief space he was standing before them telling them the things he had come to tell. It was not his message he had lacked—that had been made ready long before the hour—it was only the peculiar power and magnetism of speech and manner which had been the treasure of St. Timothy's, that he had felt himself unable to summon as he came to this humble audience. But now, as almost always, he was able to use every art at his command to capture their attention, to hold it, to carry it from point to point, and finally to drive his message home with appealing force. And this message was, as always, the simple message of belief in the things which make for righteousness.

Not all his auditors could arrive on time; they were obliged to come when they could. Brown's talks had to be subject to constant though painstakingly muffled interruptions, as one after another stole into the room. His attraction for his hearers, however, once he was fairly launched, was so great that there were few wandering eyes or minds. Therefore, to-night, when he had been speaking for a quarter of an hour, the quiet entrance of two figures which found places near the door at the back of the room disturbed nobody, and caused only a few heads to turn in their direction.

Those who did note the arrivals saw that they were strangers to the assembly. They saw something else, also, though they could not have told what it was. The two women, one young, one of middle age, were plainly dressed in cheap suits of dark serge, such as many of the working-women were wearing. Their hats were of the simplest and most inexpensive design, though lacking any of the commonplace finery to be seen everywhere throughout the room. But there was about the pair an undeniable since unconcealable air of difference, of refinement if it were only in the manner in which they slipped into their seats and fixed their eyes upon the speaker, with no glances to right or left. The eyes which noted them noted also that both were possessed of faces such as need no accessories of environment to make them hold the gaze of all about them.

"Settlement folks," guessed one girl to another, with a slight curl of the lip.

"*Sh-h—!* Who cares what they are when *he's* talkin'?" gave back the other—and settled again to listening.

Brown had seen the newcomers, but they were far back in the room, which was by no means brilliantly lighted, and beneath the shadows of their hats there was for him no hint of acquaintance. He therefore proceeded, untrammelled by a knowledge which would surely have been his undoing had he possessed it at that stage of the evening. He went on interesting, touching, appealing to his listeners, waging war upon their hearts with all the skill known to the valiant, forceful speaker. Yet such was his apparent simplicity of method that he seemed to all but two of those who heard him to be merely talking with them about the things which concerned them.

His was not the ordinary effort of the amateur social worker—such though he felt himself to be. He had not a word to say to his hearers about "conditions"; he gave them no impression of having studied them and their environment till he knew more about it all than they did—or thought he did. He brought to them only what they felt, consciously or unconsciously, to be an intimate understanding of the human heart, whether it were found beating under the coarse garments of the factory hand or the silken ones

of the "swells up-town." Gently but searchingly he showed them their own hearts, showed
them the ugly things, the strange things, the
wonderful things, of their own hearts—and then,
when he had those hearts beating heavily and
painfully before him, applied the healing balm of
his message. Hard eyes grew soft, weary faces
brightened, despairing mouths set with new re-
solve, and when the hour ended there seemed a
clearer atmosphere, a different spirit, in the
crowded room, than that which earlier had per-
vaded it.

"Say, ain't he what I told you?" One girl,
passing near the two strangers as the company
dispersed, inquired of another. "Don't it seem
like he knows what you don't know yourself
about how you're feelin'?"

"You can't be so down in the mouth when
you're listenin' to him," was another comment
which reached ears strained to attention. "You
feel like there was some good livin', after all.

Did Liz come, d'ye know?   She needs some-
thin' to make her buck up.   If she'd jest hear
him——"

Brown remained in the room till almost the
last were gone.   The two strangers waited at the
door, their backs turned to the room, as if in con-
ference.   Several women stayed to speak with
the man who had talked to them, and the waiting
ones could hear his low tones, the same friendly,
comprehending, interested tones to which St.
Timothy's had grown so happily accustomed.
At length the last lingerer passed the two by the
door, and Brown, approaching, spoke to them.

"Did you want to see me?   Is there anything
I can do?" he began—and the two strangers
turned.

His astonished gaze fell first upon Mrs. Brainard, her fine and glowing eyes fixed upon him
with both mirth and tenderness in their look.
She had been deeply touched by the sights and
sounds of the hour just passed, yet the surprise

she had in store for her friend, Donald Brown, was moving her also, and her smile at him from under the plain little hat she wore was a brilliant one. But he stared at her for a full ten seconds before he could believe the testimony of his eyes. Was this—could this poss bly be—the lady of the distinguished dress and bearing, who stood before him in her cheap suit of serge, with a little gray cotton glove upon the hand she held out to him?

He seized the hand and wrung it, as if the very contact was much to him. His face broke into a smile of joy as he said fervently, "I don't know how this happens, but it's enough for me that it does."

"I'm not the only one present, Don," said the lady, laughing, and turned to her companion.

If he had given the second figure a thought as he recognized his old friend, it was to suppose her some working-girl who had conducted the stranger to the place. But now he looked, and saw Helena Forrest.

"*You!*" he breathed, and stood transfixed.

Miss Forrest had always been, though never conspicuously dressed, such a figure of quiet elegance that one who knew her could almost recognize her with her face quite out of sight. Now, without a single accessory of the sort which stands for high-bred fashion, her beauty flashed at Brown like that of one bright star in a sky of midnight gloom. She was not smiling, she was looking straight at him with her wonderful eyes, and in them was a strange and bewildering appeal.

For a moment he could not speak—he, who had been so eloquent within her hearing for the hour past. He looked at her, and looked again at Mrs. Brainard, and back at Helena again, and then he stammered, "I can't—quite—believe it is you—either of you!" and laughed at his own confusion, his face flushing darkly under the skin, clear to the roots of the heavy locks on his forehead.

"But you see it is," said Helena's low voice. "We are confident of that ourselves, for the journey has seemed a long one, under two smothering veils. And we hadn't the easiest time finding you."

Brown recovered himself. "You didn't motor over this time, then?"

"The last time we were here," Mrs. Brainard reminded him, "you told us quite frankly that you didn't care to have your friends arrive in limousines, or in velvet and sables. So—we have left both behind."

"I see you have. It was wonderfully kind of you, though the disguise is by no means a perfect one. I wonder if you can possibly think, either of you, that you looked like the rest of my audience!"

"Did you know us when we came in?" questioned Mrs. Brainard, with a merry glance. "I think you did not, Mr. Donald Brown!"

"How long have you been here?"

"We must have come in near the beginning of your talk. You didn't even see us then, did you?"

"I saw two figures which looked strange to me —but—the lights——"

"Oh, yes," agreed the lady, gayly, "the lights were poor. And you saw two working-women who were merely strangers to you, so you didn't look again."

"I'm glad I didn't recognize you."

"Why? We rather hoped you would—didn't we, dear?"

She looked at her companion, who nodded, smiling.

"We both hoped and feared, I think," Helena said.

"I couldn't have gone stumbling on," Brown explained. "I should have had to dismiss the meeting, telling them I had a rush of blood to the head—or to the heart!"

At this moment he was helped out by the

abrupt opening of the door beside him. A
grimy-faced janitor looked in, wearing an expression of surly dissatisfaction. When he saw
Brown the expression softened slightly, as if he
knew a friend when he beheld him, but he did not
withdraw. Brown rallied his absorbed faculties
to appreciate what late hours meant to that busy
janitor.

"Just leaving, Mr. Simpson," he said cheerfully, and led his visitors out into the school's
anteroom.

"Are you at a hotel?" he asked, with eagerness, of Mrs. Brainard. "How can I—where
can I——"

"We ran away," explained that lady
promptly. "Not a soul knows where we are.
We did not register at a hotel, for this is a secret
expedition. We take the eleven-fifteen train
back. Meanwhile, Don, am I not an acceptable
chaperon? And won't my presence make it entirely proper for us to break a bit of bread with

you in your bachelor home? We had only afternoon tea before we left. We are very hungry—
or I am!"

"Oh, if you will only do that!" he said with an
inflection of great pleasure. "I shall be so tremendously honoured I shall hardly know how to
express it. I hope I have something for you fit
to eat. If I haven't——"

"Bacon and eggs," said Mrs. Brainard, with
twinkling eyes, "are what your sister Sue insists you live on. Never in my life did I have
such a longing for bacon and eggs!"

"Then you shall have them—or an omelet
garnished with bacon. And the corner grocery
has some lettuce and radishes. I believe I can
even achieve a salad."

Brown led the way through the ill-lighted
streets, not talking as he might have done in another quarter of the city, but hurrying them past
places he could not bear to have them see, and
making one détour to avoid taking them through

the poorest part of the neighbourhood. It was by no means a dangerous neighbourhood, but somehow he felt with these two rare women on his hands, as if he must guard them even from the ordinary sights to be had in the districts of the working class. And as he walked by their side it came upon him, as it had never done with such force before, that he could never seriously ask any woman from his own world to come and face such a life as the one he had chosen for the active years of his own.

Yet—he had also a curious feeling that he must not let that thought spoil for him the wonder of this visit. The hour was his, let him make the most of it. He had not so many happy hours that he could afford to lose one because it could be only one. He would not lose it.

XVI

BROWN'S NEW WORLD

So the house was reached—it was a dark and stern-looking little abode at this hour, with its windows unlighted, though usually the cheeriest on the square. Brown threw open the door and Bim sprang to meet him—turning aside, however, at sight of the strangers. Only a few embers glowed on the hearth, and the room was in darkness.

Brown closed the door behind them all. "Stand still, please," he said, "while I light up."

He threw some kindlings from a basket upon the fire, and they leaped into flame before he could light the lamp on his table. The room became a pleasant place at once, as any room must

in fire- and lamp-light, so that it contain such
few essentials of living as did Brown's—the red-
cushioned chair by the hearth, the books and
magazines upon the table, the two fine portraits
on the wall.

"Now, please make yourselves comfortable,"
Brown urged, indicating the austere little bedroom his friends remembered. "And if you'll
do that I'll go at the joyous task of getting you
some supper."

"You must let us help you," Mrs. Brainard
offered.

"Never! What could you do, either of you,
in a bachelor's kitchen?"

"But we want to see the bachelor at work
there."

"Your presence might upset me," he called
back, laughing, as he hurried away.

Two minutes later, after an inspection of his
larder, he was rushing up the street to the corner
grocery, having escaped by way of the back door.

If any of his friends of this quarter had happened to meet him under one of the scanty street lamps, they might have noted that the dark face, in these days usually so sober, to-night was alight with eagerness. Donald Brown's eyes were glowing, there was a touch of clear, excited colour on his cheek. His lips were all but smiling as he strode along. One hand was already in his pocket, feeling critically of the probable contents of the purse he longed to empty, to make a little feast for his so-welcome guests.

Arrived at Jim Burke's small store, the customer scanned the place anxiously, and it seemed to him that its supplies had never been so meagre. He succeeded in buying his lettuce, however, and a bottle of salad oil, and, remembering a can of asparagus tips on his own shelves, congratulated himself upon the attainment of his salad. Some eggs which the grocer swore were above reproach, and some small bakery cakes, completed the possibilities of the place for quick consumption. Brown ran back to the house again, his arms full of parcels, his mind struggling with the incredible fact that under his roof was housed, if only for an hour or two, the one being whom he would give all but his soul to keep.

Entering his kitchen by its outer door he stopped short upon the threshold. A figure in a white blouse, blue serge skirt, and little white, beruffled apron, was arranging his table. The table had been drawn into the middle of the room, his simple supplies of linen and silver had been discovered, and the preparations were nearly complete. In the middle of the table in a glass bowl was a huge bunch of violets, come from he could not have guessed where, even if he had given any thought to the attempt.

But he gave no thought to anything but the figure before him. If Helena Forrest, in the silks and laces of her usual evening attire, had been always one of extraordinary charm, in her present dress and setting she was infinitely more enchanting to the man who stood regarding her with his heart leaping into his throat. The whole picture she presented was one of such engaging domesticity that no bachelor who had suffered the loneliness this one had known so many months could fail to appreciate it.

He dropped his parcels and came forward. Mrs. Brainard was not in the room, and the door was closed between the kitchen and the living-room—by accident, or intention? The pulses in his temples were suddenly beating hard.

Helena did not turn. She stood by the table, trifling with some little detail of spoon or napkin, and her down-bent profile was presented to Brown's gaze. As he stared at it a sudden vivid wave of colour swept over her cheek, such an evidence of inner feeling as he had seldom ob-served in her before, who usually had herself so well in hand.

He came close and stood looking down at that

rich-hued cheek, the soft waves of her dusky hair drooping toward it.

"What does this mean?" he said, unsteadily and very low. "This can't be just to make me go mad with longing. For that's what I shall do if I look long at you like this, here in my home— *you*, looking as if—as if—you belonged here!"

He saw her hand tremble as it touched the violets in the bowl, arranging them. It was a very beautiful hand, as he well knew, and he saw with fresh wonder that there were no rings upon it, where rare and costly ones were wont to be.

There was silence for an instant before her reply. Then she turned and looked up, full into his face.

"May I belong here?" she said, very gently.

"Do you want to?"

"Yes."

"You are willing to leave it all—for me?"

"Yes."

"Ought I to let you?"

His questions had been rapid, breathless, his eyes were searching hers deeply. He was very near, but he had not put out a hand to touch her. Yet no woman, seeing him as he stood there, could feel herself the one who wooed, even though she led him on.

She looked away for an instant, while her lips broke into a little smile of wonder at his control of himself. No need to tell her how she drew him—she knew it with every fibre of her. Then she let him have her eyes again.

"Do you think you can help letting me?" she said, and lifted her face with that adorable, irresistible movement which tells its own story of its own desire.

"No!" His voice shook. "Thank God, I don't have to try any longer."

It was no passive creature he took then into his eager arms, it was one who raised her own with the rush of self-abandonment which made his joy complete. Long as he had loved her he had not dreamed of her as ever giving herself **to** any lover so splendidly. If he had dreamed— he realized with a strange feeling at the heart— he could never have withstood. . . .

It was to be hoped that Mrs. Brainard, in the other room, had found a book upon the table which interested her or, hungry for food as she had professed herself to be, she must inevitably have found the time pass slowly before she was summoned to her promised supper.

Out in the old, dark, oak-walled kitchen, Brown was still putting questions. He had placed his lady in a chair, and he sat on a little old-fashioned "cricket" before her, one that he had found in the house when he came and had carefully preserved for its oddity. It brought him just where he could look up into her eyes. One of her hands was in both his; he lifted it now and then to his lips as he talked. The packages of eggs and lettuce and bakery cakes stood un- touched and forgotten on the table. If Helena remembered to be hungry, it was not worth the spoiling of this hour to demand to be fed.

"Can I possibly make you comfortable here?" was one of his questions.

"Don't you think I look as if I might help you make us both comfortable?" was her answer.

Brown looked at the plain little white blouse, at the simple blue serge skirt, then on down to the foot which showed below the hem of the skirt.

"Is this the sort of shoe that working-women wear?" he inquired skeptically.

Helena laughed. "Neither **Mrs.** Brainard nor I could bring ourselves to that," she owned. "And since you and I are only to play at being poor——"

"We can afford to keep you in fine shoe leather? Yes, I think we can. But you are going to miss a world of things you are used to, my queen—and not only a world of things—the world itself."

"I know. But—I tried living in my world without you—and I failed."

He made an inarticulate exclamation, expressive of great joy, and followed it with the age-old demand: "Tell me when you became willing to come to mine."

"The night you were in town."

"What? Not at Atchison's dinner?"

"Yes. I would have come with you then. I would have come with you from the singing of that song."

"But you—you let me think you wanted me to come back!"

"I am only human. I wanted you to come back. But—I wanted you to refuse to come! If you hadn't refused——"

"Yes——"

"You wouldn't have towered as high for me as you do now. I might have loved you, but—perhaps—I shouldn't have—adored you!"

The last words came in a whisper, and again

BROWN'S NEW WORLD   191

the wonderful colour poured itself over her face. Brown, at the sight, bent his head upon her hand, and she put her other hand upon his heavy hair and gently caressed it. When he lifted his head his eyes were wet.

"Oh, but I don't deserve that," he murmured brokenly, and put up his arms and drew her down to him. Soon he spoke with solemnity.

"Darling, you are not making this great sacrifice wholly for me? You love—the One I try to serve? You will be glad to serve Him, too, with me?"

"Yes, Donald. But I love Him, I think, through you. I hope to reach your heights some day, but you will have to lead me there."

They remembered Mrs. Brainard at last, and they remembered that Helena, also, had had nothing at all to eat since the hour for afternoon tea. Brown flung open the door into his living-room, his face aglow, and stood laughing at the sight of Mrs. Brainard's posture in his red rocking-chair. As if exhausted by the tortures of fatigue and starvation she lay back in an attitude of utter abandonment to her fate, and only the gleam of her eyes and the smile on her lips belied the dejection of her pose.

"It's a shame!" he cried, coming to her side. "Or would be if—you hadn't aided and abetted it all."

"Are you happy, Donald dear?" asked the lady, sitting up and reaching up both hands to him. "Ah, yes; I only need to look at you!"

"So happy I don't know what I'm doing, you kind, wise friend."

"Wise? I wonder if I am. What will they all say to me, I wonder, when they know the part I've played? Never mind! Is Helena happy, too? I hope so, for the poor girl has been through the depths, bless her!"

"Come and see!" And with his arm about her, Donald led her out into the kitchen.

Helena came forward. "Dearest lady, will

"I might have loved you, but — perhaps — I shouldn't have adored you!" she said

you stay and have supper with us?" said she with quite the air of the proud young housewife, and Brown laughed in his delight.

"Had I better stay?" inquired Mrs. Brainard, laughing with the man at her side, while both regarded the figure before them with eyes which missed no note in the appeal of her presence in that place.

"Oh, yes, indeed. We've plenty and to spare. Donald paid a visit to the corner grocery not long ago, and we've new-laid eggs, and radishes and all. Do stay!"

"I think I will." And Mrs. Brainard took the radiant face between her soft, white, ringless hands and kissed it as a mother might.

In no time at all the hour had come for the visitors to go to their train. In spite of their protests Brown would have a cab come for them, though it took him some minutes to get one in a quarter of the city where such luxury was rare.

"Time enough for self-denial," said he as he

took his place facing them. "Let me play I'm a man of affluence again—just for to-night."

"I'm afraid, Don, you'll always be tempted to call cabs for your wife," Mrs. Brainard said, and suppressed a bit of a sigh; for, after all, she knew what the future must cost them both, and she herself would miss them sadly from her world.

But it was Helena who silenced her. "When he walks, I'll walk," said she. "Haven't I been in training for a year—even though I didn't know why I was training?"

"I think we've both been in training for the year," said Brown. "Even though we didn't know—God knew—and when He trains—then the end is sure!"

When he had put them in their car, and had taken leave of them with a look which he found it hard to tear away, plain and unpretentious travellers though they were that night, he went striding back through the April midnight to the little old house the Englishman had built so long ago.

As he let himself in, Bim came tearing to meet him. The firelight was still bright upon the hearth, and Brown sat down before it, leaning forward to look into the glowing coals with eyes which saw there splendid things. The dog came close and laid his head on Brown's knee and received the absent-minded but friendly caress he longed for. Also, with the need for speech, Bim's master told him something of what he was thinking.

"The look of her, Bim, boy, in those simple clothes—why, she was never half so beautiful in the most costly things she ever wore. And she's mine—mine! She's coming here—next month, Bim, to be my wife! Can you believe it? I can't—not more than half. And yet, when I remember—remember——

"And it seemed hard to me, Bim—all this year—my life here. I thought I was an exile—I, with this coming to me! *O God—but You are good to me—good!* How I will work—how we will work—*we*——".

He got up, presently, and as he stood on the hearth-rug, about to leave it for his bed, a whimsical, wonderful thought struck him.

"I'll never have to borrow little Norah Kelcey any more, for the want of something to get my arms about. Instead—some day—perhaps—*O God, but You are good!*"

THE END

THE COUNTRY LIFE PRESS
GARDEN CITY, N. Y.